LOOK BOTH WAYS

a tale told in ten blocks

also by jason reynolds

A CAITLYN DLOUHY BOOK

 ATHENEUM BOOKS FOR YOUNG READERS
NEW YORK LONDON TORONTO SYDNEY NEW DELHI

LOOK
BOTH
WAYS

a tale told in ten blocks

jason reynolds

ATHENEUM BOOKS FOR YOUNG READERS

An imprint of Simon & Schuster Children's Publishing Division

1230 Avenue of the Americas, New York, New York 10020

ATHENEUM BOOKS FOR YOUNG READERS is a registered trademark of Simon & Schuster, Inc. Atheneum logo is a trademark of Simon & Schuster, Inc.

For information about special discounts for bulk purchases, please contact Simon & Schuster Special Sales at 1-866-506-1949 or business@simonandschuster.com.

The Simon & Schuster Speakers Bureau can bring authors to your live event. For more information or to book an event, contact the Simon & Schuster Speakers Bureau at 1-866-248-3049 or visit our website at www.simonspeakers.com.

Also available in an Atheneum Books for Young Readers hardcover edition

Book design by Debra Sfetsios-Conover

The text for this book was set in ITC Stone Serif Std.

The illustrations for this book were rendered in gouache paint and digitally.

Manufactured in the United States of America

0920 MTN

First Atheneum Books for Young Readers paperback edition October 2020

10 9 8 7 6 5 4 3 2 1

The Library of Congress has cataloged the hardcover edition as follows:

Library of Congress Cataloging-in-Publication Data

Names: Reynolds, Jason, author. | Nabaum, Alexander, illustrator.

Title: Look both ways : a tale told in ten blocks /

Jason Reynolds ; illustrations by Alexander Nabaum.

Description: New York : Atheneum/Caitlyn Dlouhy Books, 2019. |

Summary: "A collection of ten short stories that all take place in the same day about kids walking home from school"—Provided by publisher.

Identifiers: LCCN 2019010095| ISBN 9781481438285 (hardback) |

ISBN 9781481438292 (pbk) | ISBN 9781481438308 (eBook)

Subjects: | CYAC: Interpersonal relations—Fiction. | Schools—Fiction. |

BISAC: JUVENILE FICTION / Social Issues / Emotions & Feelings. |

JUVENILE FICTION / Short Stories. | JUVENILE FICTION / Social Issues / New Experience.

Classification: LCC PZ7.R33593 Loo 2019 | DDC [Fic]—dc23

LC record available at https://lccn.loc.gov/2019010095

For Eloise Greenfield

LOOK BOTH WAYS

a tale told in ten blocks

WATER
BOOGER
BEARS

THIS STORY was going to begin like all the best stories. With a school bus falling from the sky.

But no one saw it happen. No one heard anything. So instead, this story will begin like all the . . . good ones.

With boogers.

"If you don't get all them nasty, half-baked goblins out your nose, I promise I'm not walking home with you. I'm not playin'." Jasmine Jordan said this like she said most things—with her whole body. Like the words weren't just coming out of her mouth but were also rolling down her spine. She said it like she meant it. Said it with the same *don't play with me* tone her mother used whenever she was trying to talk to Jasmine about something important for her "real life," and Jasmine turned the music up in her ears *real* loud to drown her mother out, and scroll on, scroll on. *If you don't take them earbugs . . . earbuds . . . airphones, or whatever they called out of your coconut head it's gon' be me turning up the volume and the bass, and I ain't talking about no music.*

That tone.

Jasmine's booger-removal warning was aimed at her stuffy-nosed best friend, Terrence Jumper. TJ. Well, Jasmine called him her "best friend who's a boy," but she didn't have best friends who were girls, so TJ was her *best friend* best friend. And she was his. Been like that for a long time. Since he moved onto Marston Street, three houses down from her. Since the only way their mothers would let them be walkers was if they walked together because they were the only kids who lived on their block. Since six years, so since forever.

The bell rang, and Jasmine and TJ had just left their last class for the day, the only class they had together. Life science with Mr. Fantana.

"You been back to school for two days and you already starting with me?" TJ spun the black lock dial confidently, like he could feel the difference in the grooves and would know when he landed on the right numbers.

"How could I not? Look at them things. Honestly, TJ, I'on't even know how you breathing right now," Jasmine continued. Their lockers were right next to each other, luckily, because Jasmine, unlike TJ, turned her lock with an intense concentration, glaring at it as if the combination could up and change at any second, or as if her fingers might stop working at any moment. And if for some strange reason either of those things happened, at least she knew TJ was right there to help.

TJ shrugged, tossing his science book onto the floor of the metal closet, the smell of feet wafting up from it like a cloud of dust, unsettled. And unsettling. The floor of his locker was littered with empty snack bags that Jasmine had slid through the door vent between classes over the last two days. Trash . . . yes. But Jasmine and TJ called them "friendship flags." The litter of love. And because Jasmine had been gone for a while, they were basically notes that said *I've missed you.* In Cheeto dust. Then, finally, with the hardened snot like tiny stones rolled in front of the entrances of his nose, TJ turned the bottom of his shirt up and mopped it. A streak of slime smeared across his lip as he swiped and pinched and dug just enough for it to count as a dig, but not enough for it to count as *diggin'.*

TJ tilted his face upward so Jasmine could get a clear line of sight into his nostrils. *"Better?"* he asked, half sincere, half hoping there was one more booger left and that it was somehow making a mean face at Jasmine.

Jasmine stared into TJ's nose like she was peering through a brown microscope of flesh, and she did this totally unfazed by the fact that TJ had just used his T-shirt—the one he was *wearing*—as a tissue. And why *would* she be bothered? Not that it wasn't disgusting (it was), but she'd known him a long time. Had seen him do things that made boogers on the bottom of a T-shirt seem like nothing more than added decoration. Booger bedazzle. A little flavor for his fashion. Had seen him use his fingers to pick gum off the bottom of his sneakers (and hers), and of course nothing would ever beat the time he clapped a mosquito dead right when it had bitten him, then licked the fly slime off his arm. That one Jasmine had dared him to do. Paid him a dollar for it. Worth it, for both of them.

"Y'know, I can see straight through to your brain," Jasmine said, pretending to still be examining. "And it turns out, there's a whole lot of it missing." She plucked TJ's nose. "Sike, sike, sike, sike. Nah, you good. I *guess* I can be seen with you now."

"Whatever." Locker slam. "I mean, we all boogers anyway."

"*You* might be a booger." Locker slam. "But me, I ain't no booger."

"That's what you think," TJ went on as they swapped backpacks. His was light. Jasmine's was packed with every class's textbook and all the world's notebooks. Makeup work. She could've carried it herself, but TJ was concerned about her back, about her muscles, because she was still recovering from the attack.

They headed down the crowded corridor, noisy with sneaker squeaks and thick with end-of-day funk. "See, I've been thinking about this. Boogers ain't nothing but water mixed with, like, dust and particles in the air and stuff like that—"

"How you know?" Jasmine interrupted. Knowing TJ, he could've heard this anywhere, like from Cynthia Sower—everybody called her Say-So—who jokes 99.99999 percent of the time.

"Looked it up online once," TJ explained. "Was trying to figure out why they so salty."

"Wait." Jasmine thrust a hand up, as if walling off the rest of TJ's words. "You *eat* them?"

"Come on, Jasmine. It ain't fair to hold my past against me. Dang." TJ shook his head. "Now, if you done interrupting, let me continue with my hypothesis." He broke "hypothesis" down into four fragmented words to put some spice on it. *High-Poth-Uh-Sis.* "So, boogers are basically water and dust." He put a finger in the air. "And human beings are mostly water, right? Ain't that what Fantana said at the beginning of the year?"

"Right."

"Okay, follow me. Every Sunday when we be at church, they always be talking about how God made us out of dust, right?" TJ and Jasmine went to the same church, where they sang in the youth choir together. TJ always asked Mrs. Bronson, the choir director, to let him sing solos even though his voice was all over the place. A set of wind chimes in a hurricane. And Jasmine's singing wasn't much better. Only difference was she knew it and would never think to ask for a solo. She loved to wear the "graduation" robes and harmonize and sway and clap, snuggling her voice into the others like drawer into dresser. Her mother always told her, *Holding a note is talent enough.*

Even though TJ couldn't hold a note—that definitely wasn't his talent—he could hold a conversation. So he continued. "God making man from dust and blowing breath into his nostrils and all that, right?"

"I . . . guess."

"You think God breath stank?"

"What?"

"Never mind. Probably not." TJ got himself back on track. "So, if God made man from dust, and now, for some reason, man—"

"And woman," Jasmine tacked on.

"Yeah, and woman . . . consist of mostly water, then basically, we water *and* dust, right?" TJ was waving his hands around like he was drawing some grand equation on an invisible board. Jasmine didn't say nothing, and she didn't need to for TJ to bring his theory home. "Which means . . . ," TJ concluded, and Jasmine could practically see the drumroll behind his eyes, "we all basically . . . boogers."

TJ wore satisfaction on his face like good lotion, and Jasmine wore confusion on hers like she'd been slapped with a gluey palm.

"Wrong," she clapped back.

"You ain't gotta believe me," TJ said, holding the door for Jasmine as they finally made it out of the building.

"Oh, I don't."

"You don't have to," TJ repeated. "But that don't mean it ain't true. See, no matter what you think I be doing in school, I really be learning. And seriously, I need to start teaching because while all these so-called scientists and teachers like Mr. Fantana be busy trying to figure out if aliens are real, I've already figured out that boogers are like . . . the babiest form of babies!"

This made Jasmine spit air. See, even though TJ was ridiculous and annoying and sometimes gross, she appreciated the fact that he always made her laugh whether she wanted to or not. Whether he was trying to or not. He was always there to chip some of the hard off. Tear at the toughness Jasmine had built up over the school year.

It had been a rough one for her.

It started with her parents separating and her father moving out. There was no drama around it. No fighting.

Nothing ugly. Nothing like the movies. At least not that she knew of. Just a really uncomfortable conversation at the kitchen table with her folks looking at her like she was an exotic fish in a sandwich bag, darting back and forth, while she squirmed in her seat as if her skin were too tight for her body.

"We love you very much."

"It's not your fault."

"Sometimes relationships change."

"Sometimes people are better apart."

"None of this is your fault."

"Your father and I love you very much."

"Your mother and I love you very much."

Actually, *that* part was just like the movies. Especially the ones about girls her age. The kitchen-table conference. The follow-up knock-knock on the bedroom door. The kid cussing at the dad. The mom saying, "Language!" The weekend visits. The awkwardness of both parents asking if everything is all right,

over and over and over and over and over and over again.

And that was just the first quarter. That was before she had her worst attack. And not an attack by someone else. She ain't get jumped or nothing. Instead her body attacked itself. Jasmine had a blood disease since birth—sickle cell anemia—which can affect almost every part of the body. Organs, joints, even vision.

But for the most part it hadn't given Jasmine any real problems. A little pain sometimes, but nothing too bad until this year when she went into full-on crisis and her body became a blaze. At least that's what it felt like. Her hands and feet swelled like plastic gloves full of water, heavy and tight, ready to burst. Her muscles felt like they'd become wood and she imagined her bones were splintering and growing bones of their own.

Jasmine was out sick for a month. Her locker unopened. The lock, unturned.

Her mom and dad, together and apart, weirdly hovering over her hospital bed like aliens from movies even cornier than teenage family dramas. Her parents' coldness thawed by the one and only TJ, who would show up, crack some jokes, break some ice, and leave some empty potato chip bags next to Jasmine's bed to add to the thirty he'd left in her locker. Friendship flags.

And when Jasmine finally returned to Latimer Middle School two days ago, after being jumped with questions from classmates who'd almost never spoken to her before she got sick—people who looked at her sideways for being so close to TJ because "boys and girls can't just be friends"—Jasmine (and the guidance counselor, Ms. Lane) had to figure out how she was going to catch up on her work. Couldn't do it while she was laid up because she could barely move. It hurt to hold a pen. Hurt to turn a page. Which was how she knew she wasn't a booger. Couldn't have been a booger. She wasn't gooey enough.

Maybe all *boys* are boogers. Always acting like rocks when really y'all just blobs of dusty water," Jasmine joked as she and TJ crossed at the light, the crosswalk like a bridge leading them over the tar-water, from school to neighborhood. They turned down Portal Avenue, a route they'd taken hundreds of times. A route TJ had been forced to take alone for the last month. And even though Jasmine had been at school yesterday, her mother had been too nervous to let her walk on her first day back. So this was their first day walking home together again. "But not me," she continued. "I mean, come on, boogers get wiped away, get blown out."

"Okay, so if you ain't no booger, then what are you?" TJ asked.

Jasmine shrugged. "Um . . . a girl? I'm me."

"Come on, Jasmine. Work with me here." Now TJ was spreading his arms. Talked with his body like an old street hustler trying to convince people that stolen goods are a steal. "If you ain't no booger, but you *had* to be something else, what would you be?"

Jasmine thought about it as they turned left down Marston, a street lined with houses that her mother always said had been around for a long time. *An old neighborhood*, she'd ramble whenever they drove through newer, seemingly nicer communities, where every house looked like the last house, like a choir of homes dressed in the same robes, turned the same way, singing the same melody in the same key, which makes for a boring, boring song. But Marston Street was lined with a little bit of everything, from small brick to fancy vinyl. From bay windows to Colonial style. From ramblers all on one level to three stories. A fence here and there, a gate there and here. Grass. Gravel. Blacktop. Pavement. Everything old enough to look lived in. To look tried on. Old enough to be warm and worn by a generation or two. Maybe even three.

"I don't know," she said at last. "I mean, what was that thing Mr. Fantana was talking about in class today? The thing he pulled up the picture of? I mean, it kinda looked like a booger."

"You talking about that ugly slug-looking thing? What he call it . . . a space bear?"

"Yeah," she started, then stopped. "Hold up. . . . First of all, I ain't no ugly thing. Just so we clear. But I'm that. A *water* bear." Jasmine nodded.

"Yeah, water bear," TJ said, chuckling. "That thing got like eight legs and it got them long nails like my old mother. And that weird mouth . . . like my old mother—" TJ poked his lips out, then pulled them in, then poked them out and pulled them in again as if he were chewing on a giant piece of bubble gum. "That thing would be super scary—like my old mother—if it wasn't so teeny-tiny, which definitely *ain't* like my old mother. At. All."

"Ms. Macy not scary, boy."

"Ms. Macy ain't my old mother. She my new mother. And my *mother mother* I don't really know like that."

"Right . . . right." Jasmine tried to keep all the mothers organized in her head. A different equation on a different invisible board.

"But my *old* mother . . ." TJ let the thought trail off, shuddering like something shot through his body. Just for a moment. A bad memory, maybe. "Anyway, why would you want to be *that* thing? The water bear or whatever. Can't nobody even see it. At least we can *see* boogers."

"Because of what Mr. Fantana was saying about how scientists tested that little water bear thingy, and they found out it might be the toughest living thing in the world. In the universe maybe. Said it could survive the hottest heat. And the coldest cold. And the pressurest pressure. I mean, they sent it into space—*SPACE*—and it came back just crawling around like ain't nothing happen. Just crawling crawling. That's me all day. With nails intact." Jasmine huffed on her fingers and pretended to buff the purple-painted tips.

"Yeah, if you believe all that, I guess."

"Well, if you can believe God made us out of dust—which I believe because you definitely the dustiest person I ever known—then I can believe Mr. Fantana about this water bear. Shoot, we probably be stepping on them every day and don't even know it."

TJ looked quick down at the ground, suddenly wondering what lived between the cracks in the concrete. Scratched his arms like maybe the water bears were crawling in the crevices of his dry skin and he didn't know because he couldn't see them. Jasmine watched him fidget. Huh. She'd never really witnessed him nervous. TJ wasn't afraid of boogers, dog poop, eating bugs, or anything like that, but maybe that's because he could see them. He could smash and smear and disappear them. But it dawned on her that he seemed freaked out dealing with the things that wouldn't smash or smear. The things already invisible living all around him, and maybe even on him, and there was nothing he could do about it.

They got to TJ's house. No gate, no fence. A patch of dry grass. The house was small and wooden like it had been built without machines. No bulldozers or anything like that. Just human hands and love and hammers and nails and more love. There was a hole in the screen door that had been there for years. TJ's foot had done that. He said sometimes his feet get mad and do things like kick or stomp or run. Don't blame him, he'd say. And Jasmine would laugh because his jokes were always funny even though she knew they were almost never jokes.

They sat on the steps out front, bumped shoulders, and talked more about water bears and boogers and decided that maybe they could be both.

"Water bear boogers?" Jasmine suggested while tying her shoes.

TJ offered a slight adjustment. "How about . . . water booger bears?"

"Ah, water booger bears." Jasmine perked up, nodded. "I like that."

The door opened behind them, the screen screeching a striking impression of TJ's voice.

"I thought I heard something out here." It was his (not-so) new mother. His mom of six years, Ms. Macy. She was dressed in her work uniform—navy pants, navy shirt with a name tag, offset by her fuzzy, dingy pink house slippers. She bent down and kissed both Jasmine and TJ on the tops of their heads, the remnants of her day now hovering around them like hard-work halos. "How was school?"

"Fine," TJ said, smirking, sniffling, scratching.

"Pretty good," Jasmine confirmed.

"That's what I like to hear," Ms. Macy said. They knew what was coming next. "So . . . what y'all learn today?" Even though Ms. Macy asked this question—the *same* question—every day, her voice was still so interested.

Jasmine looked at TJ. He looked back at her, a new booger resting in his left nostril. It seemed to have appeared out of nowhere, like boogers often do. He wiped it with the back of his hand and they both chimed in unison, like a Sunday choir.

"Nothing."

THE LOW CUTS
STRIKE
AGAIN

ALL I CAN tell you is if you ever see John John Watson, Francy Baskin, Trista Smith, or especially Britton "Bit" Burns—the Low Cuts—better watch your pockets. Those four, they'll steal anything that jingles, even your hands if you got them tucked and they're making too much noise. Matter of fact, they'd take the pockets out your pockets if they could. Once they walked into a convenience store, one of the ones with the dish at the front of the counter that says TAKE A PENNY, LEAVE A PENNY and took all the pennies.

Leaving no pennies.

A *grab and get gone.*

Okay, they didn't do that just once. They did that *all* the time. They did it so much that store owners started keeping the dish behind the register and doled out the pennies to short-changed customers individually. Other times, Bit, Francy, John John, and Trista would challenge people to quarter wars, which is when two people stand quarters up on a desk or a table and spin them like spinning tops. Whichever quarter knocks the other quarter over, or lasts the longest, wins. But the rules don't really matter to this crew. The opponent's quarter was getting pinched or the opponent was getting punched. And twenty-five cents ain't worth a swole-up eye.

But the Low Cuts don't just take to be taking. They don't steal for fun. Actually, they don't even like doing it. But they do it because they have to. At least they feel like they have to. Before they named themselves the Low Cuts, they were part of another set that they had no choice but to be down with. The free-lunchers. Sounded much cooler than it was. It didn't mean they got free lunch because they were special. Or because they were popular and loved so much that the school cafeteria offered them mozzarella sticks and crinkle-cut fries on the house. Instead, what it meant was their parents were tight, hard up, squeezed, strapped. Their folks didn't have any extra scratch to give for the itch of hunger. No lunch money. And that was true for each of the Low Cuts. Wasn't something they were proud of, or something they were ashamed of either, even though other kids tried to make them feel a way about it.

"Yo, if I give you my pizza crust every day and you save it up, you'll have a whole loaf of bread by the end of the school year" was a joke told by a kid named Andrew Knotts, who, after Bit heard it . . . let's just say Andrew never cracked those kinds of jokes again.

For the record, Bit, John John, Francy, and Trista weren't the only free-lunchers, but they were the only free-lunchers with parents who were cancer survivors. They'd been put together in an in-school support group run by the guidance counselor, Ms. Lane. Sitting in a circle passing a tissue box back and forth, talking about how hard it is to watch your parents skinny up, watch their hair thin and fall out, watch their bodies turn disloyal. How scary it was to think about whether or not their mothers and fathers were going to live, and if not, how they were all going to live without them.

What the four of them never talked about was how all the surgeries and treatments were what knocked everything in their lives and their parents' lives off track financially. It was where all the money went. That wasn't Ms. Lane's job, to bring that up. Not part of the kumbaya circles that Bit pretended to be too tough for. And the truth is, they wouldn't have known any of this if Bit's mother hadn't told him all her business. But she did. And Bit told that business to the others.

And the others asked their parents if it was true.

"That's not for you to worry about," John John's mother said. Breast Cancer.

"Who told you that?" Francy's father asked. Prostate Cancer.

"I . . . We don't want to lie to you," Trista's father explained. Stomach Cancer.

True. True. True.

And it was this, not the cancer but the strain it put on everyone, that formed the Low Cuts. They all cut their hair down to almost bald—a sign of solidarity—and started stealing.

There was only one rule:

Only take loose change. No dollars. No jewelry. No wallets. Only change.

Usually they used it for extras at lunch.

Today it was for something else.

The sound of the bell ringing, signaling the end of the day, might as well have been a starter pistol or an air horn. Something to make the Low Cuts go. And go they did. They burst from their classes—Bit and Trista from English, John John from math, and Francy from Spanish class. After stopping at their lockers, swapping books, packing bags, they burst from the school and gathered at the meeting place.

There were three benches to the right of the double

doors. The first was being babysat by some boy in a uniform holding a broken skateboard across his lap, stroking it like a hurt dog. The second was occupied by Gregory Pitts and his friends swatting their arms through a cloud of body spray that smelled like cinnamon if cinnamon smelled like garlic. And the third bench was where the Low Cuts always met. A base chosen by Bit.

Bit was the tiniest person in their crew. And the obvious leader. He was always going on and on about how his growth spurt was going to come soon and then he'd be the tallest, but nobody believed him. And even though Bit was half the size of his friends, he was the biggest when it came to confidence. And when it came to temper. He was known for knocking people out. There was a kid named Trey who was picking on John John, calling him an old man because John John had a patch of gray hair in the front of his head. He was born with it. A birthmark. Teased for it his whole life. Funny thing was, the gray patch, when cut low, looked more like a ringworm and would've made for much better jokes, which were the jokes Bit would've cracked if John John weren't his Low Cut brother. But Trey wasn't that sharp.

"John John, you was born a senior citizen," Trey said.

"John John, you look like you getting ready to retire from middle school," Trey said.

"John John, soon you gon' need a walker to be a . . . walker," Trey said.

"John John—"

That was the last *John John* Trey spoke before Bit's *fist fist* went in his mouth so *fast fast* it knocked him *out out* in the middle of the crosswalk. Thankfully the crossing guard, Ms. Post, was there to wake Trey up. And while she was helping, Bit took off running.

He'd done the same for Francy when boys were picking on her for having short hair, calling her *Franky*, but she never paid them no mind. It never really bothered her. Francy always had a way of ignoring that kind of thing. The bigger person and all. But not Bit. Bit would knock heads, no question. And if no one was around, he'd pat their pockets after putting them to sleep. But only for loose change. Of course.

Trista wasn't the type who needed any kind of puff-up from Bit. She was the kind of girl nobody messed with. Nobody. She could slice you to slivers with one sentence. Plus she was a daddy's girl, and he raised her up in martial arts. *Tae Kwon Do Trista.* Everyone had seen her do a roundhouse kick at a school talent show, and that was enough for no one to ever try her. Including Bit.

The four of them together were the kids teachers were concerned about. The ones they talked trash about in the teachers' lounge. The ones they marked as "at risk." They were the ones Ms. Wockley would wag her finger and shake her head at whenever they walked down the hall or sat together and had secret meetings at lunch. The way they were—a braid of brilliance and bravado—concerned everyone.

"Everybody ready?" Bit asked, one foot on the bench, huddling everyone up. Trista was the only one not paying attention. She was talking to a boy who responded awkwardly, like he was scared or something. No surprise. "Trista." Bit shot her a look.

"Ready, ready." Trista joined the fold, slipping her phone from her back pocket to check the time. "It's 3:16."

"Truck comes in an hour," Francy announced.

"Let's see how much we got," John John said, opening his hand. Some dimes. A nickel. Everyone else dug in their pockets and dropped their findings into John John's cupped palm. A few more nickels. Some found in the change slots of the lunchroom vending machines. Others found deep in the pockets of unsuspecting skinny boys wearing unforgiving skinny jeans. Quite a few pennies found swept into the corner by Mr. Munch, the school's janitor. These had to be sifted out from dust bunnies, gum wrappers, and hair ties. Nickels and dimes swiped from teachers' desks. Only from the top. Never from the drawers.

No quarters on this run. Unfortunately.

Trista moved the change around with her finger,

counting. "Seventy, eighty, eighty-five, eighty-six, eighty-seven, eighty-eight, eighty-nine . . ."

"Ninety?" Bit asked, his eyes darting from John John's palm to the double doors. Ms. Wockley was always too close for comfort.

"Yeah. Only ninety cents," Trista confirmed, counting it all again. She turned to Bit, who was rocking back and forth, anxious. "Think that's enough?"

Bit spat. "We'll make it work." He marched off and the others followed behind, worming through the crowd and up to the light. They crossed and headed down the main road—Portal Avenue—cars and bikes zooming past. Buses, both public and school, grumbling and screeching, smoke billowing from the tailpipes.

Even though they were tight on time, they were loose on talk. Francy, in particular, was motor-mouthing— she always did when she was anxious—asking John John if he'd ever heard of anybody named Satchmo, because there was a kid in her Spanish class named Satchmo Jenkins, and she just liked the name.

"Nope. Never heard of nobody else named Francy either though," John John said with a shrug.

"Yeah, but Francy is short for Francis," she went on.

"Well, maybe Satchmo is short for . . . Satchmo . . . . *reece* . . . Maurice . . . Satchmaurice . . . Satchmo . . . Satchmocha . . . Satchmocha latte . . . Satch . . ."

"Satchmo *Money*," Bit sparked, annoyed by the silly

conversation Francy and John John were having, and also by the silly conversation Trista was trying to have with him.

"Bit, I'm serious," Trista was droning on. "What you gonna write about being?" Trista was referring to their English homework. Ms. Broome wanted each student to write about being something else. Not a person. A thing.

"I keep telling you, Trista. I don't know," Bit replied as a school bus rumbled by. "How 'bout a school bus? That good enough for you?"

"Not really," Trista said. The school bus was coming to a stop, its brakes grinding. Bit covered his ears.

"I hate that sound. Matter of fact, I'd be a school bus that could fly. That way I ain't gotta hit the brakes and make all that noise." Bit looked over at Trista. "How 'bout that?"

"All I'm gon' say is, I could totally see you, a school bus falling from the sky." Trista laughed to herself, but just loud enough for Bit to hear.

"Well, at least then I'd be a rocket."

After six blocks they turned down Crossman Street, stopping at the first house. The one that sat on the corner. An older house with a bunch of cars parked in the yard. Barrel grills and Big Wheels in the driveway. A mess, but the home of the munchie master, Ms. CeeCee.

Ms. CeeCee had been the neighborhood candy lady

since the Low Cuts' parents were kids. She was known for making sure everybody got a fair shot at sweet treats because she knew not everybody could get to the corner store. There wasn't one on the corner of Crossman. Actually, there wasn't one within five blocks. So she had to be it. And the best part about Ms. CeeCee was that she was open twenty-four hours a day.

With Bit leading the way, the Low Cuts beelined up her obstacle course of a driveway and rang the doorbell, which chimed a melodic yawn, like an old man just waking up. The Low Cuts waited nervously. But Bit, full of fire and impatience, rang the bell again.

And again.

"Come on," he growled. "Ain't nobody got all day."

"Chill," Francy said. "You know she move slow."

Sure enough, a few seconds later they heard the sound of Ms. CeeCee's slippers slowly sliding across the floor and her voice oozing through the wooden door. "I'm coming. I'm coming. Don't poop your pants."

Trista smiled at that because Ms. CeeCee always mentioned pooping as if the only people who ever rang her bell were people in desperate need of a bathroom.

The door swung open, and there she was. A small lady, jet-black wig sitting on top of her head like a hat she'd purposely cocked to the side. The hair was too dark, especially compared to the few silver hairs springing from her chin. She wore a turquoise sweat suit, the sleeves and legs cut off, threads hanging like a blue-green spiderweb. Her ankles were swollen, and so were her cheeks. If it weren't for the hair and the bumpy freckles, her face would've looked like a baby's. Her voice, on the other hand, sounded like a truck engine.

"Look who it is: Eenie, Meanie, Minie, and Mo," Ms. CeeCee said, pointing at each of them. "What y'all want?"

"Well," John John started, because John John was usually the one who spoke for the crew. The nice one. He dug in his pocket, opened his hand showing all the silver and copper. "We got ninety cents, and—"

"We need candy, Ms. CeeCee," Bit blurted. Then, clapping his hands together, he repeated, "We . . . need . . . candy."

"Bit." Francy's voice was a warning to calm down, but Bit's ears didn't hear it that way.

"What? We *do*. And we in a rush!" He tapped his wrist where there was no watch. Checked it like checking a pulse. A live one, for sure.

"Don't be rude," Trista said, calm. Like, too calm. So calm that even Ms. CeeCee took a step back. Bit quieted down. Huffed, rolled his wrist, and muttered, "Go 'head, John John."

"We got ninety cents and we need as much candy as you can give us," John John explained.

Ms. CeeCee looked at the four of them, a stairstep from John John, the tallest, down to Bit.

"Do I want to know what y'all up to?" she asked, and they just looked at her like she hadn't asked it. Like she hadn't said anything. So she acted like she hadn't said anything either. "Wait right here."

The thing about Ms. CeeCee's house was that kids could never go in unsupervised. Even though she knew them and their parents, she was always very careful about young people in her home buying candy because it basically was the plot of every abduction story she'd ever watched, and she didn't want people thinking she was doing that. Because she wasn't. So the Low Cuts had to wait at the door another few minutes until Ms. CeeCee returned with a small card table. She set the table up just outside the house, then pulled boxes of candy from a small closet right by the front door, where most people would hang their coats.

She set the boxes up on the table.

"Okay, today in the penny, nickel, and dime categories, we got the old stuff."

"You always say that when we come here. Don't nobody want no stale candy, Ms. CeeCee," Bit said, fighting himself to cool his tone.

"It's not stale, Britton. It's just older styles of candies. Like how them Michael Jordan sneakers y'all be paying all that money for keep getting remade? That's what this is. Retro candy. Hard to get, and used to cost only a penny a piece when I was a little girl, but I gotta charge y'all four cents more. Attitude tax." Bit cocked his head. Ms. CeeCee cocked hers right back. "Let that be a lesson, son. Plus, everything costs more over time."

"Inflation," Francy said.

"Sounds more like deflation," Bit grumbled under his breath, patting his pockets.

"What you say?" Ms. CeeCee asked, adding the last box to the lineup on the table.

"Nothing," John John subbed in for Bit.

"Okay, y'all know the rundown," Ms. CeeCee said. "I got Mary Janes. Tootsie Rolls. Squirrel Nut Zippers—"

Bit did his best to trap his laugh, but a *pfft* slipped from his mouth. No matter how tough and tight he was, Squirrel Nut Zippers broke him every time.

"Let her finish," Francy said, through her own giggles.

"Squirrel Nut Zippers," Ms. CeeCee repeated, then continued with the list. "Life Savers, individually wrapped. Bit-O-Honey, Charleston Chews, Bazooka bubble gum, and . . ." She popped back into the closet, mumbling to herself, then popped back out. "I think that's it, in terms of bang for your buck."

They leaned over the table looking at all the candy, trying to decide which was the right candy to get. Finally Francy spoke up.

"What you think, Bit?"

"Oh, *now* y'all care what I think," he snapped back.

"Don't be petty all your life." That was from John John.

"We just know you know what to do with it better than us," Francy explained. "You know . . . how to . . . use it."

"Exactly," Trista said, scratching her head.

Ms. CeeCee covered her ears. "I don't wanna know. I don't wanna know."

Bit turned to her. "I mean, you said this candy from when you were young, right?"

Ms. CeeCee pulled her hands away from her face. "That's right."

"So which was your favorite?"

Ms. CeeCee surveyed the table. "Hmm. It'd have to be a tie between the Mary Janes and the Life Savers. I mean, that peanut butter mixed with syrup in the Mary Janes was like heaven. But the pure sugar of the Life Savers was to little Cecelia, a life saver."

"So, we'll take as many of both of those as we can get."

Ms. CeeCee started to count them out, and a few seconds later there were eighteen pieces of candy in front of them. Nine Mary Janes. Nine Life Savers.

John John lets the coins fall into Ms. CeeCee's hands, Bit scooping up the candy.

"Later, Ms. CeeCee," he said, already walking away.

"Boy, one of these days you gon' learn some manners," she clapped back. "Tell your mama I'm praying for her. Matter of fact, I'm praying for all your mamas. Knuckleheads."

"Low Cuts," Francy said, smiling.

"Right, Low Cuts. Short Cuts. Whatever. You'll always be knuckleheads to me."

"Come *onnnn.*" Bit was at the end of the driveway, rocking back and forth, antsy. "We running out of time."

They went back to the main road. Back to busy Portal Avenue with the cars and trucks and other kids—other walkers—lollygagging on their way home from school. "What's the math, Francy?" John John asked as he pulled a wad of sandwich bags from his pocket.

Francy was the smartest Low Cut when it came to numbers. She could break it all down in her head in a way that would've taken Bit and John John a calculator to do, and Trista probably two pages of long division.

"Eighteen pieces. We do bundles of three. That's six bundles. Sell them for a dollar a pop."

"That's only six bucks," Bit said.

"Yeah, and that's enough," John John replied.

"No. We need more. We can get more." Bit had turned around and was walking backward so he could look his friends in their faces. "I know these guys. I mean, I know these *kinds* of guys. They don't carry change. Ever. So we charge them $1.50 and they'll give us two. Matter of fact, because we don't even have time for all these transactions, let's just do three bundles of six. Two fifty a pop. They'll all pay three, and—"

"We'll walk with nine." See, even though Francy was the best with math, Bit was the best with hustle. No doubt about it.

When they got to Placer Street—which they'd practically run to after figuring out the numbers—they stopped on the corner, out of breath, and organized the candy. Three Mary Janes and three Life Savers in three bags.

Trista slid her phone from her back pocket again. "It's three forty-four. We got fifteen minutes."

"Gotta make this quick," Francy said, twisting the bags, tying knots at the tops of them.

A block down the street they came up to a building that looked like an old house but had a sign out front. **PLACER POOL.**

The Low Cuts stood outside, stared at the building for a moment, working up the nerve to go in. And whether the nerve was worked up or not, once Bit said, "Ready?" he took off for the door. It chimed when he pushed it open and stepped into the smoky building, John John, Trista, and Francy following close behind.

Silence, except for one pool ball smacking against another. Then total silence. Old men, like scraggly human cigarettes with non-human cigarettes dangling from their mouths, all turned and looked. And after a few awkward seconds, Bit ballooned his chest with bravery, rolled his shoulders back, and said, "Candy for sale."

A man came from behind an old wooden bar. "Kid, you can't be in here." Bit knew he couldn't be in there. He knew none of them could be in there. But he had been watching this place for a while. He'd been sitting across the street checking out who was going in and how long they stayed. The smoke that came screaming out every time the door opened. The cussing men who went on about losing money and the laughing men who bragged about winning some. This was a place for pool players, but more than that, Bit knew it was a place for hustlers.

"Don't I know you?" another man said.

"Don't matter if you know me," Bit shot back. "Me and my friends selling candy. Say buy or say bye." John John, Trista, and Francy were impressed by that line. They'd heard Bit talk like this before. This wasn't the first time they'd done this. They'd walked into a bingo hall once and heard him tell an old lady he was her troll doll, the only good luck charm she'd ever need. But this time was different. There was a knife in his voice. Something sharp they'd never heard.

And the guy did know him. Knew him from the neighborhood. That guy had fixed his mother's car once. And Bit had stood next to him, mean-mugging the whole time the guy was under the hood just in case he tried to cheat his mom.

"We don't want no candy. So how about—"

"We got Mary Janes and Life Savers." Francy joined in, held the bags up like they were full of gold coins.

"Yeah. We got Mary Janes and Life Savers," Bit said, doubling down.

"Mary Janes?" a man wearing an eye patch called from the back of the room. He set his pool cue down on the table next to him and walked toward the Low Cuts. "What y'all know 'bout Mary Janes?"

"We know we got 'em. And Life Savers, too."

"Individually wrapped," John John added, just because it was a detail Ms. CeeCee kept adding.

The man chuckled. "I can't remember the last time I had a Mary Jane." He slapped the guy next to him. "You?"

"Been a long time. Used to go down south to visit my grandpappy and he'd always have that kind of stuff in his pocket. Be all melted and still be good. And Grandma used to give us strawberry candy, and when she ran out, she'd give us cherry Life Savers."

"And them butterscotch." Another man.

"*Whew*, and don't get me started on them, uh . . . them Squirrel Nut Zippers." This came from the guy who ran the place.

"All this is great, gentlemen . . ." Bit put a pothole in

the middle of memory lane. "But like the man said, we ain't allowed in here, so—"

"How much?" Eye Patch asked.

Bit turned and looked at his friends. Bounced his eyebrows just slightly. Just enough for them to see.

"Bundles of six. Three of each candy. Two fifty."

"Two fifty! That's penny candy! At least it was when I was coming up." Eye Patch couldn't believe it.

"My mother said gas was a dollar when she was a kid," Bit shot back.

"And I heard Jordans cost, like, eighty bucks," John John followed, again stealing Ms. CeeCee's line. "Guess everything costs more over time."

The Low Cuts, in what seemed like one fluid motion, all shrugged.

"I'll tell you what ain't never been cheap—kids," Eye Patch said.

"And I'll tell *you* what's hard to find—Mary Janes," one of the other men said, digging in his pocket. He clearly had no idea that there was a woman who sold them right around the corner. "You said two fifty?"

"Yeah," Bit said, bouncing on his toes, anxious.

"You got change?"

Bit looked at his friends again. Bounced his eyebrows again. "Nope."

The man pulled three bucks from his pocket. Handed it to Bit. Francy handed over the first bag.

Trista spoke up. "Thank you."

"Hey, I took them dollars off him," he replied to Trista, but pointed to a red-haired man, who just laughed and muttered something they couldn't hear. "Eight ball, corner pocket. *Cha-ching!*" The buyer pumped his fist.

And that was it. The last two bags were snatched up immediately, because it turned out, the thing about men in pool halls is none of them want to be outdone. For John John, Francy, and Trista, it was like looking at a roomful of bigger Bits. In the future.

Nine dollars later, the Low Cuts were out the door and almost out of time. Trista didn't bother checking her phone. They knew they were late because they saw the ice-cream truck pulling off from its usual post, in front of the fifth house on Placer Street. It hadn't been there when they'd gone into the pool hall—it arrived at four every day—and never stayed if kids weren't waiting there to buy anything—gone by 4:02.

It was 4:03.

So they ran.

All four of them broke out down the street, sprinting, screaming for the ice-cream truck to stop. Halfway down the block, it finally did. The Low Cuts ran up to the truck, slapping their hands on the side of it. The driver yanked the window open.

"Almost missed me," the ice-cream man said. He

looked more like somebody's big brother than an ice-cream man. "What can I get for y'all?"

"Four vanilla soft serves," Bit ordered.

"Cup or cone?"

"Cup."

"Sprinkles?"

Francy, John John, and Trista looked to Bit.

"Hmmm, sure," Bit said.

"On all four?"

"Yep." Bit didn't ask anyone else. And no one contested.

The ice-cream man handed cup after cup through the window, rainbow sprinkles all over them. Bit passed them down so that each of the Low Cuts had one, then handed the ice-cream man the nine dollars.

"It's only eight," the ice-cream man said.

"A dollar for you," Bit replied. "Thanks for stopping."

As the ice-cream truck pulled off, John John, Trista, Francy, and Bit walked a few houses down, until they got to a small house they'd all been to before. That Trista and Francy always called cute, John John never called nothing, and Bit called home. Bit pulled his key out of his pocket, unlocked the door.

"Ma!" he yelled. "You dressed?"

Seconds later, Bit's mother, Ms. Burns, came from the back and was greeted by all of them—the Low Cuts—holding cups of fresh ice cream. Not one swirl licked.

Not one spoonful missing. Ms. Burns looked at them, her face both cloudy and sunny, her skin absent of her normal brown.

Bit's mom had relapsed.

The cancer had come back, but the doctors were optimistic she could beat it again.

"Hey. What's going on? How was school?" Bit's mother asked, kissing him on the forehead. But he shrugged off the question.

"How was your first day back on chemo?"

"Oh, it was . . . you know. It was chemo. I'm okay." But she sounded exhausted and rubbed her stomach. "A little queasy."

"I figured you would be. So, we got you a bunch of ice cream." Bit waved his arm like a game show host showing off the four cups. "Vanilla," he said. The other Low Cuts watched Bit the hustler, Bit who could turn ninety cents into nine bucks—into ice cream—turn into a son. A son who was scared. A son who loved his mom.

And she smiled, her shiny eyes jumping from face to face, bald head to bald head, friend to friend.

"With sprinkles."

SKITTER
HITTER

MAYBE IF Pia Foster had known yesterday, when the bell rang and she ran to her locker, grabbed her skateboard, and started kicking down the hall of Latimer Middle School—the wheels rolling and scratching over the floor sounding like the *chugga-chugga* of a small train— that the journey home would be different, she wouldn't have been in such a hurry. Maybe she wouldn't have ignored her classmates moving out of the way, sucking their teeth all annoyed by her decision to dart through the crowd as if riding on an arrow no one wanted to be struck by, shot from a *get out of school* bow no one could see. Maybe she would've excused herself. Apologized for almost clipping ankles or running over toes. Maybe she would've walked. For once. Maybe even stayed after and talked to Fawn Samms, the only other skater she knew. The only other skater who was a girl. The only other skater she respected. Maybe Pia would've tightened wheels with her. Talked about deck art, stickers, sneakers. Maybe practiced tricks in the parking lot after all the buses were gone. Heel flips. Kick flips. Maybe watched videos on their phones. Videos of Santi hitting ollies in a dress and pumps. Maybe Pia would've even told Fawn about her. About Santi. About what happened to her. Fawn would've listened. Might not have said nothing because Fawn don't talk much either. But she would've listened, for sure. Heard her. Maybe Pia would've done all this. Or maybe not. Maybe if she wasn't so soft-spoken. But she was and the skateboard, like so many skaters', was her voice at its loudest saying, *Get out the way or pay!*

She named her board Skitter. And called it "she."

Maybe if Stevie Munson had known yesterday the skateboard's name was Skitter, he would've said something. Maybe if he'd known Pia's name was Pia. If he'd known she had a big sister named Santi. Maybe if he'd just known those things, he would've done something. Something different. Something at all.

The bell rang at Brookshire Boys Academy, and an ocean of testosteronies crashed into the hallway, green ties swinging like polyester tails coming from their throats. Matching pants and blazers. White dress shirts with soggy collars from all the neck sweat and faded red splotches on their chests from the ketchup that missed their mouths. But Stevie's shirt was stained from lots of things: food, sweat, Magic Marker . . . Marcus.

Marcus Bradford was a box-faced baseball player who wrote stuff on the back of Stevie's shirt almost every day. Stevie was a sweater, so he always took his blazer off in class to avoid becoming a washcloth— something to wring out. But the oxford button-downs he wore underneath the blazer were all two sizes too big because his mom couldn't afford to buy new ones every year. School was already expensive enough, so the uniform, he'd have to grow into. "Everything will fit eventually," his mother would say, but the fabric was always so blousy and poofed away from Stevie's body in a way that made it impossible to feel Marcus's pens and markers gliding across the cotton. So Marcus used Stevie's shirts like locker room walls, for jagged graffiti and curse words.

And maybe if yesterday Pia had known his name— Stevie—maybe if she had shaken his hand and said, *My name is*, and he'd said, *My name is*, she could've read his face. Read his fear. Maybe he could've read hers. Or maybe not. Either way, Pia would've taken her house key from around her neck and clutched it with the teeth jutting between her fingers. A fist-knife. Just in case.

Maybe Stevie wouldn't have been there at all yesterday, with Marcus and the boys, if he hadn't tried to figure out a way to get them to leave him, and his shirt, alone. Telling wasn't an option. Snitches get stitches and sometimes ditches. That's what Marcus said the other day when Stevie found out Marcus had drawn a green penis on the back of his shirt. *Greenis* written underneath. Maybe Stevie wouldn't have even been there with them if his mother hadn't asked him what he was doing with all the bleach. Why was he using so much of it?

"Not that I'm not glad you're washing your own clothes, but detergent and bleach ain't free," she'd say. And what Stevie couldn't say was, *I'm sorry, but there's a boy in my school drawing on my clothes,* because then his mother would say, *I don't send you to private school for boys to draw private parts on your private uniform that you still have to grow into,* and *Do I need to call the principal?* and Stevie didn't want to hear none of that. Stitches, remember? Maybe even ditches. Besides, Mr. Brock, the principal, already knew. He'd seen the pictures and words and all he ever said was, *Boys will be boys.*

But whether Stevie told his mother about Marcus or not, yesterday Pia still would've taken that way home. She still would've kicked down the hall, dashing through the crowd on her skateboard, ignoring all the teeth smacking and slick talk and Ms. Wockley yelling, "No skating allowed!" Feeling that freedom she was used to. The kind of freedom that comes from feet not touching the ground. Coasting through the school door, weaving and winding across the pavement, riding the asphalt wave, avoiding the bus waiters and the pickup parents. The orange sashes of safety patrols and the sound of a whistle blown by the crossing guard. A whistle Pia never listened to because skating meant freedom. Rules were for the classroom, where teachers would say things like *Participation is part of your grade.*

But Pia wasn't a participator. Not in school. She spent most days daydreaming about frontside 180s, while scribbling her sister's name on the desk—the *S*, a geometric trick that looked more like a pointy eight, the way Santi always wrote it—and thinking about how much it sucked to roll an ankle, and yet rolling an ankle was way better than Ms. Broome calling Pia's name to ask her to explain what some old guy she never heard of meant in a story she'd never read but was supposed to read just because Ms. Broome said she was supposed to read it. Pia was always ready to go. To cut into the wind and float down Portal Avenue toward Bastion Street. Pit stop at the skate park. Skate down Santi's sidewalk. Roll toward home.

Stevie was never ready to go. Because to go meant to get got by Marcus and the boys.

There was one time they grabbed Stevie by the tie and yanked it so hard that his neck was sore for a week. They called it "Snatch the tail off the donkey." The triangle knot had been pulled so tight that undoing it was like trying to unravel a rock. So he cut it off, buried it in the bottom of his backpack, a dead fabric snake. Told his mother he lost it. And she lost her mind.

"I don't send you to a private school for you to lose ties. I send you there for you to be able to make them one day!" she yelled. But she knew her son. Knew he was the kind of kid who could lose the brown off his skin if he closed his eyes for too long.

Another time when Stevie wasn't paying attention, Marcus and the boys ran up on him and threw a cup of water all over the front of his pants. Then they cupped their hands around their mouths and announced to as much of the world as possible that Stevie had pissed himself. And even though Stevie said he hadn't, pleaded it like his life depended on it, they talked over him, howling and shrieking, *Yo, you pissed your pants! Everybody, this fool pissed himself!* Stevie was so embarrassed that he almost matched their joke with the real thing.

And then there was the time Marcus decided he needed to practice his wrestling moves. The ones he watched on TV. And who better to practice on than Stevie? Kid never saw it coming. A body slam. An elbow drop. A pile driver. A pin on the sidewalk, one, two, three, while the other boys threw their hands up and cheered like audience members and taped the whole thing on their phones. *Viral.*

So Stevie was never ready to go. Until yesterday when Marcus and the boys finally offered him . . . freedom.

Pia saw them. Yesterday. She was used to seeing them and they were used to seeing her, but they never said nothing. Normally they stepped to the side and let Pia skate by. It was usually only three boys standing along the fence at the skate park, but this time, four. Dressed in green. And if Pia hadn't known Marcus, she would've thought private school guys were automatically good. She would've thought their ties made them mature. She would've thought they lived perfect lives, in perfect neighborhoods, in perfect houses with clean windows and green grass. Grass even greener than their jackets. Houses that smelled like coffee in the morning and popcorn at night.

But she knew Marcus.

Marcus's mother owned the salon Pia went to whenever her mom made her get her hair done, which was mainly for holidays when they would have to go to her grandmother's for dinner. And her mother had learned a long time ago that the only way to get Pia to go to the salon without kicking was to let her take Skitter the skateboard with her. Let her kick that around the parking lot until it was her turn in the chair so that Pia wouldn't have to sit for hours flipping through old magazines filled with fancy advertisements of stick-figure models with bodies pretzeled up, printed on paper that smelled like the perfume Santi wore. When she was smaller, Pia would sniff the pages, and once— when the salon was really backed up—she sniffed and sniffed until the strange mixture of glue, ink, and flowers made her nauseous. She puked all over the salon floor. That was when her mother had finally given in and allowed her to bring the board with her.

At first, whenever Pia'd skate back and forth across the parking lot outside the salon, Marcus, who was always pouting while sweeping up the hair inside the salon, would come out with her. One time, he asked if he could ride Skitter. Pia kicked the board over to him. Marcus put one foot on the deck and steadied himself. And as soon as he lifted the other foot, the board flew out from under him. He caught air before slamming to the ground, only to find that his pants had split up the middle and his superhero briefs were on blast.

But Pia didn't laugh. Instead, she tried to help him up. But he couldn't take her hand, cover his butt, *and* wipe his eyes at the same time. He never came outside with her again except for one day, years later. And on that day, he didn't speak to her or ask to ride her skateboard. He just sat on the curb and watched but pretended he wasn't watching as Pia kicked harder than usual, sailing over the asphalt, grinding her board against the curb, scraping it like she hated it, almost violently. Attempting tricks she knew she couldn't do, rocketing to the ground over and over again. Then getting back up, getting back on, ignoring Marcus's fake chuckles.

She could never forget that day. It was the day she was getting her hair done for her sister's funeral. A jacked-up French roll with what felt like two hundred bobby pins that started itching as soon as she left the chair.

Pia felt that same itch when she saw Marcus and the boys yesterday. When she saw the knots at their throats and felt a knot in hers. Because she knew Marcus. She knew where his mother's black eyes were coming from. Where her swollen jaws and forehead lumps were coming from. Because that same day Pia sat under the dryer two years back, after her wash and before the French roll was put in, she heard her mom ask Marcus's mom when she was going to leave Marcus's father. With the dryer whirring in Pia's ears, it sounded like the two women were whispering in a tornado. But Pia could still hear them through the storm.

"I ain't trying to get in your business, Lydia. I swear. And if you tell me to mind my own, I will. I mean, with Santi's death and *this one* here, I got more than enough to mind. But I can't sit here and pretend like I don't see what I see. And I'm definitely not 'bout to act like I don't care about you, Lydia. You *and* Marcus. So, I gotta ask you, before this man kills you, when you gon' leave?"

When Stevie realized, yesterday, that the girl skating down the street was going to be a target, and that target would be the ticket to him being left alone by Marcus and the boys—accepted as one of them—he got nervous. Nauseous.

"What . . . what we doing?" He choked on his words.

"Just playin' a game," Marcus said, grabbing Stevie's shoulder like a baseball to be fastballed at Pia. But Stevie had a curveball in mind. Told Marcus he wouldn't do anything to her.

"I don't want you to do nothing to *her*," Marcus scowled. "Just take her skateboard. That's all."

The boys lined up, became a wall on the sidewalk, and Pia thought about hopping the curb to go around them but knew better than to skate into oncoming traffic. She'd cut it close before. Too scary. So Pia reluctantly put a foot down, dragged her sneaker along the concrete to slow down, then stomped the back of the skateboard, flipping it up into her hand.

"'Scuse me," she said politely to Marcus.

"Excuse you," he said back, puffing his chest. Pia never looked down. Looked each boy in the face. Each of them looked back, except for one. The new boy,

Stevie, looked everywhere else. To the left, to the right, up and down. Anywhere but at her. "Let me borrow your board?" Marcus said. "Just for a second. My man been working on a trick and he wanted to show us." Marcus nudged Stevie.

"He don't look like he skate," Pia said, sizing Stevie up.

"I bet he skate better than you." Marcus stepped toward her, yanking Stevie with him.

Stevie looked like he was two seconds from vomiting the bones out of his body, leaving him as nothing but a skin suit lying on the sidewalk.

Pia could smell Stevie. A punchy musk, stronger than the perfume in the magazines. He was sweating through his blazer. And before he could answer, Marcus reached for Skitter, grabbed the board, and yanked it. But Pia wouldn't release it. After a back-and-forth—Pia gripping the board with both hands—Marcus tried a different approach. He let go, and Pia stumbled back but didn't fall. Balance. But Marcus was right there to do gravity's work. Shoved her to the ground. The skateboard flew from her hands and skidded into the street, where a car, horn blaring, rolled over it.

"Ohhhh!" The boys howled as the wooden plank split, their stupid excitement splintering Pia's skin.

Her voice cracked, broken in half.

She got up and ran. Mind racing. Thinking. About Santi.

Stevie chased behind her.

Pia ran faster. Thinking about Santi. How she was pushed off her board by a boy.

Stevie stopped running.

Pia ran home. Thinking about Santi. How the boy was just mad Santi was a better skater than he was.

Pushed her into the street. Thinking about himself.

Oncoming traffic.

Had Stevie known that's what it would take to be one of Marcus's boys, he wouldn't have come yesterday. Or maybe he would have, but he would've said something. Would've stopped Marcus. Why didn't he say anything? Why didn't he stop it? That's what he asked himself as he walked back down the sidewalk. That's what he asked himself when he tipped into the street, his hand up timidly as traffic slowed for him, and picked up the cracked halves of the skateboard. He held them like he was holding a broken heart, looked around only to find that Marcus and the boys had left him. Like the suckers they were. Like the sucker he was.

And maybe if Pia had known Stevie had picked up the pieces of her board, maybe if she'd known that he took them home with him, maybe if she'd known that he finally told his mother about Marcus, told her where all the bleach was going, why he had to wash his clothes every day to try to remove the stains and marks and words inked into his uniform, showed her the tie he'd cut off his neck and hid in the bottom of his bag—the one he'd said he'd lost—explained why he hadn't had an appetite, why his grades were slipping, maybe if Pia had known that he told his mother what he'd just done, what he didn't do, what he'd just seen, maybe if Pia had known that his mother struggled to hold back a scream, helped him tape the deck back together, punished him, sent him to bed, woke him up early this morning for extra chores, maybe if Pia had known that his mother, after meeting with the principal, pulled Stevie out of school early, drove him to what they guessed was Pia's school—the only public middle school in the area—sat stuck in traffic lecturing him, paying no attention to the news on the radio (a school bus had fallen from the sky!), made him stand outside the entrance and wait for Pia awkwardly, maybe if Pia had known that Stevie was coming to apologize for his silence, maybe, maybe, maybe, just maybe Pia wouldn't have left through the back door.

Today.

With Fawn. To walk to the cemetery to visit Santi's grave and ask her questions, hard questions, about boys.

HOW TO LOOK
(BOTH)
BOTH WAYS

FATIMA MOSS talks to only one person on her way home from school. And before she talks to that person she keeps a checklist of all the things on her journey that have changed. And all the things that have stayed the same. That one person and their sameness or differentness included.

This is that checklist.

1. Bell rings for five seconds.
2. Twenty-eight students (twenty-nine, including me) dash from Ms. Broome's English class.
    Difference: Today, Trista Smith and Britton Burns ran faster than everyone.
    Almost knocked Sam Mosby over.

3. I take off.

4. The whole school crowds into the hallway.

5. It's so noisy I can't hear myself think.

6. I stop at my locker to get this notebook, which I keep there where it's safe. So I can hear myself think.

7. The combination to my lock is the same.

8. I get it wrong.

9. I panic and think someone has switched my lock, which means I may never get my notebook.

10. I try the combination again and it works.

11. The combination to my lock is the same.

12. I grab this notebook, get the books I'll need for homework, which is usually none because I usually get all my homework done before school is over.

    Difference: But today I have homework. English. Ms. Broome wants us to imagine ourselves as objects. Any object we want. And write about it.

    Doesn't require a book though.

13. I head from my locker to the school doors. Between seventy-seven and eighty-four steps, depending on if Ms. Wockley is yelling at anyone in the middle of the hallway. Today she was yelling at Simeon

Cross for running down the hall with Kenzi Thompson on his back. Again. (Technically not a difference.) Today it took eighty-one.

14. Exit the building. The double doors are always open.

15. Six school buses out front. Two lines of cars for pickup. Mr. Johnson is directing traffic.

16. Between eighty-six and ninety-four steps to the corner where the crossing guard, Ms. Post, stands.

17. "Hi, Fatima," she says.
Difference: Today she said, "Hey, Fatima."

18. Ms. Post's son, Canton, sits at the stop sign on the corner holding a broom. With no broomstick. It's weird. But not weird because he's always there.

19. I keep walking straight. Don't have to cross the street.

20. I count the signs (already one stop sign), hydrants, and major cracks in the sidewalk. Not all the cracks. That would be too hard. Too many. But the big ones.

21. Don't walk too fast. Have to take note of all the houses too. How they look.

22. They all look the same. They all look like

they're made of graham crackers. They all look like the houses I drew when I was like six. Box with a triangle on top. Except bigger. They all have big windows. I think they all have beige carpet inside. And a front room no one sits in.

23. I know there are nineteen of these houses from the crossing guard's corner to my house.

24. My house is number twenty.

25. My house looks exactly the same as the others. It also has beige carpet inside. And a front room no one sits in.

26. Because of that, I don't really have to pay too much attention to the houses. I can just count the signs.

27. SCHOOL CROSSING is the first sign. A picture of an adult and a child. I think. Weird, because kids cross by themselves.

28. Look both ways.

29. One-way sign. Right at the beginning. Always there. I still look both ways.

30. The speed limit is fifteen. There's a sign that says so.

31. There are four stop signs. One at the end of each block.

32. There are five houses on each block. I don't

know any of the people who live in any of them. That's the same.

33. I wonder if any of them see me walk past every day with this notebook. If they count me and say, same.

34. I wonder if all the houses are empty like mine. People have to work to pay bills. Graham cracker houses cost a lot of money, I think. So does green grass. And bushes. And people who cut that grass and trim those bushes.

Difference: There's a chunk of roses snatched out of House No. 8's rosebush. Doesn't look like a mistake either.

35. I've been counting cracks. I've learned to look up and down at the same time. Look both ways.

36. By the time I reach House No. 8, I have stepped over only six cracks in the sidewalk. Six big cracks. Big enough that if you don't know they're there, you will trip.

37. I meet Benni at the same place I meet her every day, the same place I met her months ago, doing what she does every day and was doing months ago. Singing.

Benni Austin sings old songs like they're new songs. She also does old dances like they're new dances. Wears old clothes like they're new clothes. Fatima met her on her first day as a walker. Fatima's mother and father had given her strict instructions on what to do and which way to go, easy instructions to follow because Fatima only had to go straight. One way down Portal Avenue. No stopping. No talking. Eyes up, looking both ways. Eyes up, which is why Fatima tripped on one of the six big cracks where the sidewalk split—a lightning bolt of a separation—one part lifted just enough to be annoying. And dangerous. Fatima stubbed her toe, then went flying but only after a few stumbles and bumbles and stumble-bumbles, like her mind was trying to convince her body to stay grounded but her body wouldn't be held down, wanted to leap, wanted to catch air.

Her body won.

She took flight.

But only for a second.

Then she took . . . fall.

Fatima crashed onto the sidewalk, the skin on her knees scraping off into stinging red strips. It was the kind of fall that requires a person to lie still for a moment, let the experience wash over them like a wave of boiling water. So Fatima lay there for maybe six seconds, which were five seconds too many because a bus had pulled up and had stopped at the stop sign.

And as Fatima heard the clacking sound of the windows on the bus lowering—*clack, clack, clack, clack, clack*—Fatima knew that fifteen miles an hour would be much slower than she'd thought it would be. That it was more like five miles an hour. No miles an hour.

"*Wowwwww!*" a boy from the bus yells. This was followed by a series of other cornball zingers involving *eating it, biting it,* and *dive after five,* even though it was just past three in the afternoon.

"Pay attention, or you'll lose your life!" one kid yelled. All Fatima remembered about that kid was his lisp, that the "th" he put on "lose" made it sound like *looth,* and the spit that flew from his mouth, big enough for Fatima to see it. But it was the kid behind him who caught her attention even more. A boy who sat in his seat with the window up, thick ropes of hair sprouting from his head like antennae. He held a notebook up to his face, peeked over it at her, and she could tell that behind that notebook he wasn't laughing. Not at all.

By the time the bus passed her, Fatima had started to get up. Her knees were buzzing, bloody, and each move, each step made her draw in short gusts of air.

And then she heard a long drawling voice, the kind of voice that was deep for no reason. The voice was singing. Singing in a tone that most would consider *sanging,* but it wasn't exactly good. Or bad. But enthusiastic and better than the bus, that's for sure.

"Get ready!" the voice, attached to a woman, sang-shouted. She was bopping up the street, pumping her arms as if banging on the biggest invisible drum set ever imagined. Offbeat. Not a big woman. Not too small either. Just somewhere in the middle, which was the only way she could've (barely) fit the blazer she had on. Green. A school patch sewn on the breast pocket. It was filthy. White shirt, wet with sweat. Soft pink pants with creases so sharp down the front that it looked like she could cut the air with each step. *"I'm mad! That's a fact. Get READY for the big payback."* And then in a higher tone she repeated, *"The big payback!"* Then . . . spin move.

Fatima, unsure of who this lady was or what she was about, jumped up, grabbed her backpack, and limped on. And the lady limped on too, right next to Fatima, and screamed again. *"Get ready!"* She noticed Fatima flinch.

And stopped.

Stopped singing.

Stopped dancing.

Stopped walking.

Just stopped, dead in her tracks in the middle of the sidewalk, her face becoming loose, sloshy.

That afternoon when Fatima's parents came home from work, they were ready to ask about her first walk home but noticed her hobbling. Fatima had already cleaned the wounds with alcohol—*yikes!*—and put Band-Aids on both kneecaps.

"Why are you walking like that, Fati?" her mother asked as Fatima inched her way into her mother's hug.

"I tripped on the way home. Landed hard," Fatima explained, still a little embarrassed. "And there was a bus full of kids who laughed," she went on, but she left out the part about the woman in the pink pants because she knew that if she told her mother, her mother would tell her father, and that would be the end of walking. That would be the end of a babysitterless life. Back to cheese-toast snack time and other coughy kids whining about what they want to watch on TV. And she didn't want that because even though the first walk was rough, anything was worth trying again if it meant she could come home and be alone in her house, where she could microwave nuggets and pretend to be a flight attendant like her father.

A life jacket is in the pocket under your seat. To put it on, place it over your head. Clip on the waistband and pull it tight. Please do not inflate it while you are still inside the aircraft. An evacuation slide and life raft are at each door. Your crew will direct you to your door. Additional emergency exits are shown on the leaflet.

In case of emergency, oxygen masks will drop down in

front of you. Please pull the mask down toward your face and place the mask over your mouth and nose. If you are traveling with a child, please attend to yourself first, then the child. Breathe normally.

She'd had that memorized since she was little. She'd heard her father say different versions of it through the years, whether it was, *In case of emergency, the bath water is in front of you. Please pull your washcloth down toward your face and scrub over your mouth and nose.* Or, *Please do not poop while your butt is still in the underwear. An evacuation slide and life raft are at each door. And by that I mean, use the toilet.* Then he'd do the two-finger point to the bathroom.

"I keep telling you, you have to pay attention, sweetheart," her mother said now. "You have to look both ways and all ways. That even includes, despite what your dad says, down."

The next day, Fatima looked down the whole time. Studied the ground with such concentration she didn't notice the clouds forming above her head. The rain came almost at the exact spot where the crack was that had clipped her the day before. Came by the bucketful. Drenched her in seconds. And as the same bus crept by, the same kids smashed their faces to the glass. They laughed and pointed again. Predictable. The boy with the lisp splattered spit on the window, wiped it clean with his sleeve. The boy behind him sat with the notebook up to his face again. No jokes in his eyes.

And the singing lady was there. Came bopping down the street like it wasn't raining. She was singing, but the rain was louder than her voice. This time she was wearing a tuxedo and a top hat and was carrying a closed umbrella.

She extended it to Fatima. "You play guitar?" she asked.

"Huh?" Fatima was confused. There was no guitar.

"Do. You. Play. The *gee*tar?" she asked again, this time strumming the closed umbrella. And before Fatima could answer, the lady said, "Yeah, you do. You play it. I can always tell. *Ha!* Benni can always tell!" The lady—Benni—extended the umbrella again. Fatima took it this time, opened it. And Benni said, "*Woo!* Sounds *amazing!*" bobbing her head and snapping her fingers to nothing. "It's your solo! Go, go! Put on a show for the people!" Benni stopped walking, waved, and cheered for Fatima, who played nothing. Just held the umbrella over her head and walked faster.

"Nothing changes, Fati. At least nothing major," Fatima's mother explained that evening over dinner. She worked as some kind of environmental scientist, so everything for her was like this. "If you see clouds, expect rain. If you see cracks, lift your feet. If you see houses, expect them to be the same houses every day, because houses don't move. They don't change."

"Routine lessens risk," her father chimed in, scarfing his food because he had a flight to catch.

Routine lessens risk. And Fatima was tired of the risky stuff. The tripping. The rain. She needed this walk home to be one she could predict so that she could get there safely. That night she thought about the boy with the notebook. The one on the bus sitting behind the spitty one. She thought about how he hid behind the spiral and lined paper. How it somehow made him feel safer. Less . . . out there. At least that's what Fatima thought. So she decided to use a note- book to try to do the same. To write down things in her life so she could pay attention to how they stayed the same and know whenever they changed so that she could be ready for what that change might bring. Her mother did this all the time with her experiments. Always taught her to do this with her science projects over the years.

"In order for us to know how these plants grow in natural sunlight, as opposed to how they grow under the house lights, we have to write down every single constant and every single variable, then record all prog- ress. Every leaf. Every inch. Every day," she preached, just a year before all this.

So the next day, the moment the bell rang, Fatima's data collection began. An ongoing list of things that almost never changed. The bell. The hallway. The locker. The lock. The door. The corner. The crossing guard. The houses. The signs.

And the singing lady, Benni, who since then has stayed the same in that she's changed every. Single. Day.

37. (Cont.) Today Benni's dressed in a black wig. The hair is straight and falls just to her chin. She has on a sky-blue dress. And combat boots.
Difference: She's singing a song that goes "Runaway child, running wild, better go back hooooome, where you belong."
Difference: She's doing dance steps. One looks like she's shoveling the ground. Like she's digging.

38. I speak to her.

39. She speaks to me. Calls me "Fatima the Dreamer." Says "Dreamer" like "dream-uh."

40. I ask how she's doing. She says fine.
Difference: She tells me she saw a school bus fall from the sky.

41. She always says stuff like that.

42. She asks me if anything's different today.

43. I tell her about Trista Smith and Britton Burns running out of class faster than usual. And how I have homework. I have to imagine myself as something else, for Ms. Broome's

class. Also, pointed to the roses missing from House No. 8. Thought Benni would pull one from behind her back or from under her wig, which is something Benni would do. She'd probably call it a microphone.

44. Benni nods.

Difference: And started mumbling, "But how you gon' change the world? How you gon' change the world?"

45. Benni walks with me.

Difference: Now screaming, "How you gon' change the world? How you gon' change the world? How you gon' change the world?!"

46. I ignore Benni. I keep counting the houses.

Difference: Benni won't stop. This is not a song.

47. I keep counting the cracks.

Difference: Benni is still screaming as the bus drives by. Screams, "There it is!" But I don't look. I don't want to see if anyone is laughing at Benni. At me.

48. I keep counting the signs.

Difference: I can barely hear myself think. Even though the signs have been there every day.

49. I stop at House No. 15. One block from my house. Usually where Benni leaves me.

Difference: Benni runs in front of me.
Leans against the stop sign and asks,
"Fatima, I'm serious. How you gon' change
the world?'"

50. I look both ways.

Difference: Then I think about Ms.
Broome's assignment. What could I be?
What do I wish I could become to change
the world? I think about telling Benni
I might want to be wet cement to fill
the cracks in the sidewalk. Not to hide.
But to stop someone else from tripping.
Or maybe I'd be an umbrella to keep rain
from someone's head. Keep someone dry in
a storm. But I don't say none of that
to Benni, because I don't think either of
those things would change the world. So I
tell her I don't know.

I don't know. I don't know how to change
the world.

Then ask her if she'd maybe let me borrow
one of her instruments to play.

BURMAN ST.

CALL OF
DUTY

BRYSON WILLS didn't go to school today. His mother let him stay home, not because of all the pain in his face—the black eye, the busted lip, the swollen jaw, the scrapes—but because she figured it was a good idea to let things cool off. To put some space between him and what happened. To let the situation breathe. Before she left the house she told Bryson a bunch of things—that she loved him and was proud of him, but most importantly, that he shouldn't play video games all day. Bryson's father came in his room after his mom and told him the same things, minus the part about video games.

"Love you, Bry," his dad said, kissing him on the cheek over and over again like he did every morning, until Bryson grunted something that his father translated as, "Love you too." Then Bryson rolled over, his plush mattress suddenly prickly like a bed of nails against his bruised body.

A few hours later, Bryson was awake, standing, yawning, stretching—all of which felt like he was pulling himself apart. He eased down the hall into the kitchen, microwaved a bowl of oatmeal, poured a glass of apple juice. Then sat in front of the TV, where, even though his mother said not to, he'd planned to play video games. Allllll day. He didn't want to think about school. Or after school. The walk home. None of it. But he couldn't help it. The thoughts were there like the smell of coffee that seemed to linger in the house long after it had been brewed.

Bryson chewed his lumpy oatmeal slowly, choked it down, replaying the scene. The moment that landed him there with a body on fire. The punches thrown, the kicks kicked. Everyone's phones out, recording. He'd seen the clips all over social media the night before. Commentary. Filters. Memes. Hashtags. #BurmanStreetBeatdown. The shaky footage of him throwing haymakers, trying not to fall, because once you fall, it's over. Everyone knows that. Ain't no getting up. Ain't no coming back.

He signed out. Then signed back in. Then deleted all the apps from his phone. At least for a few days. He wouldn't have—he wouldn't have been able to—but his mom made him. Made him unplug from the laughs and likes. From the catchy captions and antics from kids who barely spoke in school but had mastered saying the right things online, matched with the perfect light and angle to turn out-of-this-world boredom into an Oscar-worthy blockbuster. And now Bryson was sitting alone on the living room floor, trying to swallow sludgy oats and forget it all.

By going to war.

The television glowed.

Call of Duty.

Xbox, powered on.

Headset on.

Controller gripped,

as Bryson Wills crawled into World War II.

Ty Carson went to school today. And the whole time he was there he felt like he was being watched, stared at even though the new rumor had taken over yesterday's old one. Because rumors only last a day. But still, Ty felt like his classmates were following him. Not stalking him, peeping around corners and things like that. No. But more like looking away whenever he'd catch their eyes. Or cutting their conversations whenever he walked by, like he was some kind of human mute button. Made him paranoid. So paranoid he even felt like every clock was actually a giant eye, and every time the bell rang he imagined it was the building laughing at him. He was losing it and wished he could make himself small. Unseeable. Turn himself into a speck. Into a black streak swiped across the floor from a sneaker sole. Turn himself into a penny swept into one of the corners by Mr. Munch's big broom. But he couldn't do none of that, so he shrank mentally. Tried to crawl inside himself, another thing he wished he could *really* do. Be like a turtle. Pull his head into the home of his body. Look around the shell. Try to figure out why he felt how he felt. Why he did what he did, which was nothing but felt like something. Yesterday. Figure out if it was wrong. It wasn't wrong. But maybe it was. He didn't know and that was the hard part. Or at least part of the hard part. About yesterday. Not just yesterday, but yesterday . . . too. Yesterday when everything was fine. Yesterday when he could just be . . . Ty.

Ty was cool enough to be cool with everybody, because most people looked at him like a human video game. Bright. Full of color and sound. Awkward movements. Dramatic moments. He lived in his own world, but it was a world full of windows that everyone could see into. A world full of *bloops* and *bleeps*, *vrooms*, and the occasional *boom*. It wasn't strange to see him pretending to crawl up the lockers, or for him to perform tactical movements like barrel rolls in the middle of the hallway. The type of kid who wore his backpack on the front of his body—a chest pack—just so he could pretend it was some type of armor, and on any given day an umbrella could become either sword or shotgun. And to top it all off, Ty was one of the best gamers around. Nationally ranked. And everyone knew. He'd won tournaments and competitions and had been trying to get Ms. Wockley to convince Mr. Jarrett to start a gaming league at the school.

"We don't need more distractions, Mr. Carson," she'd say, biting down hard on her words.

"*Bleep, bleep, bleep, bloop*, Ms. Wockley," he'd reply. He'd shake his head and she'd shake hers, and that would be that.

Because everyone knew Ty's gaming skills, his classmates were always trying to convince him to play on their squads, but Ty only played with the best. Well, he *was* the best so . . . the second best. And at their school, the second best was Bryson Wills. A boy whose father made him grow out his hair, and instead of letting him get it braided or cornrowed, convinced him that an Afro was the best way to go. And Bryson owned it. He owned it so much that his screen name was AfroGamer. Ty's was TYred, which he said was pronounced "tired" because he was *so tired of beating everyone.* But most gamers thought it was TY Red, which made sense too, because Ty saw red whenever he was playing. All instinct. All thumbs.

Bryson and Ty lived close enough to each other to get together on weekends and play. Sometimes, Bryson would come to Ty's house, a small house over on Crossman—Bryson liked this because Ms. CeeCee, the world's best candy lady, lived at the top of Ty's street— and other times Ty would come over to Bryson's house, a bigger house over on Burman. Ty preferred to play at Bryson's. The snacks were better. The TV was bigger. And a tiny dog named Max Payne wasn't running around barking and clawing at it.

The game of choice: *Call of Duty, World War II*, which really bothered his parents.

"*Pac-Man* . . . now, that's a game. You just eat and run away from ghosts, which is what I like to call, life," his father said, joking.

"Or *Super Mario Bros*," his mother added. "I mean, other than fighting the big bosses, you're basically just trying not to be eaten by the environment. Mushrooms and plants and . . ."

"Turtles!" his father yipped.

"It's nothing like what you're playing."

Ty tried to convince his parents *Call of Duty* was educational. That it was basically like interactive social studies class. That there was no better way to learn about that particular war than to jump right into it.

"There is *no* way you can know war, son," Ty's mother scolded. "Not unless you've fought in one. And you haven't. You're talking about *Nazis*. That's a lot more than some video game."

Ty understood that he didn't know the kind of war he was simulating in the game. That his controller wasn't a rifle and his raggedy family-reunion T-shirt wasn't a flak jacket. His headset wasn't a helmet, and the sounds in his ears were, in fact, just sounds in his ears. But Ty also knew that there *was* some kind of war he was in. Some kind of battle he did know but couldn't make sense of. That the other sounds in his head were more than just sounds, that they made his heart do weird things, made his stomach tighten. Ty knew the anxiety of a kind of war. He knew the adrenaline and the confusion of it all.

Because yesterday. Because yesterday. Because yesterday.

Ty had been kissed. By a boy. Slim.

At the water fountain after first period. PE.

On his cheek.

But close enough to his mouth to count.

They were fighting over the water.

We were fighting over the water, right?

It was weird.

He was surprised. But not mad. Which was more surprising.

It was so weird.

It wasn't that weird.

It was a little weird. But not a whole lot weird.

It was seen. By someone no one saw see it.

And that someone told everyone. Everyone.

And by lunch, Slim—whose real name was Salem—had twisted the story, told everyone Ty kissed *him*. So when Ty walked into the cafeteria, he walked into a minefield. A war zone. Everyone locked and loaded, firing at him.

Bryson had heard the rumor. It snaked around, passed from mouth to ear, a hiss-whisper. It eventually came to Bryson through Remy Vaughn. If Remy didn't try to act cool, he probably would've been the coolest kid in the school. But . . . nope.

"So?" Bryson shot back, slamming his locker door.

"So, that mean he gay."

"No it don't," Bryson said, annoyed. "And even if it do, so what?" Bryson swung his backpack onto his shoulder watching Remy's face, trying to work out why he cared so much about Ty and Slim. So Bryson asked him. "Why *you* care so much?"

"I don't."

"You do. I mean, here's a better question. How many girls have *you* kissed?"

"I don't know, a bunch," Remy said, looking off. Bryson knew that was a lie and that he hadn't kissed anyone. And Bryson didn't hold that against him because he hadn't kissed anyone either. But he never lied about it. It was no big deal. Plus, why lie to a person you know knows the truth? Remy's best friend Candace was Bryson's cousin, and she was always going on and on about how Remy was forever acting like some kind of lover boy that no one's ever loved.

"Right. A *bunch*. I guess negative numbers are still numbers," Bryson razzed. "I just think it might be best to mind your business." He patted Remy on the shoulder and walked away.

In the cafeteria, instead of people leaving Ty alone, instead of them cracking their stupid jokes to each other, a bunch of them had decided they'd sit with him. Crowd around him at the lunch table. Tease him to his face. Including Slim.

By the time Bryson got there, they were calling Ty all kinds of names. Names that bite. Names that stick and mark. Names that catch fire and leave a burnt smell in the air. The boys mocked him, bending their wrists as if they'd just shot a basketball and were holding the follow-through. Holding. Holding.

"Yo, what's goin' on?" Bryson asked, coming up to the table. He stood behind Ty, his hair like an eclipsed sun. "Scoot over, Ty. Lemme slide in." Ty inched to the left and Bryson sat next to him, set his tray of mozzarella sticks on the table. "What's everyone talking about?"

"Oh, nothin'," Slim said. "Just that Ty tried to kiss

me because . . . he's gay!" He said it like it was a *your mama* joke. Like he'd just chopped Ty down. Ty shook his head like it didn't matter, but Bryson could tell it did. It for sure did.

"Hmm, interesting," Bryson said, looking down at the fried cheese fingers on his tray. "Because I heard *you* kissed *him*." He glanced up at Slim.

"Because that's true," Ty confirmed, relieved Bryson was there. His backup, just like in the game. *Watch my back. Cover me, cover me!*

"That ain't true!" Slim barked, looking around to make sure everyone heard him. "I wouldn't kiss no boy!"

"Hey, hey, hey, man." Bryson put his hands up. "If you did, you did. It's all good. I mean, you might wanna ask permission next time instead of just sneaking it. That's a little weird, but . . . relax." The other guys at the table didn't know if they should laugh or *ooh*, or nod, or what. They couldn't tell if Bryson was being serious or if he was joking around.

"You talking like you like boys, too," Trey Larson, a fake tough guy who everyone knew got chumped by the smallest kid in the school, said to Bryson. Bryson started laughing.

"Am I? I think Slim is. Matter of fact, I think all y'all are." Bryson pointed at all the jokesters. "Like my father always says, 'Those that scar you are you.'" He checked their faces, and it wasn't hard to tell that they had no idea what that meant. He looked at Ty, and Ty's face looked no different. A gem dropped in the mud. "The point is, I don't like boys. Not like that. But I like Ty." He patted Ty on the back. "Matter of fact, I like him more than I like y'all, and for real for real, I don't see what the big deal is. A kiss on the cheek? That's what all y'all roasting him for? A kiss on the cheek? Really?" Bryson looked at Slim, held his eyes there for a while before looking at the other guys. "That's *it?*"

And then.

Bryson leaned over and pecked Ty on the cheek. *Mwah'd* and all. Then put his eyes right back on Slim.

"Look at that. I'm still . . . alive." He made his voice sound ghostly, shrugged, then ate a mozzarella stick. The table fell silent. Well, at least to Bryson and Ty. They wouldn't have known if the other boys actually stopped talking and joking because they were no longer paying attention.

But attention would be paid. And it would be paid to Bryson. Because for the remainder of the afternoon, the rumor had become different. It had transformed. Switched from Ty kissing Slim, to Bryson kissing Ty, the mighty snake of gossip going from a harmless garter to a venomous python. Bryson did his best to ignore it all. To think about it as a stage in a game, a board beaten only by making it to the end of the day bell.

But as soon as that bell rang and Bryson left school, he noticed that Slim and some of the other boys were following him down Portal Avenue. Bryson knew they were trailing him because he'd never seen them walk this way before and was pretty sure they didn't live on his side of the neighborhood. He could hear them laughing. Hear them yelling things, and even though he couldn't make out what they were yelling, he could still feel the sounds of their voices pricking him like staples in the back.

As soon as he turned down Burman Street, Bryson could hear their feet quicken, hear the footfalls on the pavement speed up like rain going from drizzle to downpour. And instead of running, Bryson just turned around, put his hands up, and did his best.

That was yesterday, and today, at school, Ty heard the whispers. The python had become a boa, strangling him. Wrapped all around his body, squeezing him, squeezing. Crushing his lungs and heart. The whispers did nothing but confirm what he'd already known. What he'd already seen online the night before. The rumors that Slim and Andrew and whoever else they were with had jumped Bryson. That Bryson had held his own as best he could, but there were four of them. That they were calling him everything but his name. So in Mr. Davanzo's last class of the day, when the bell rang, Ty ran.

He ran out of class. He ran down the corridor. He ran

through the double doors. He ran past Ms. Post. He ran down Portal Avenue as fast as he could for as long as he could until he was out of breath.

Then he walked. Fast. And stopped only when he got to a house a few blocks before Burman Street. A big beige-colored house with a big window. Beautiful green grass and shrubs that outlined the yard, accented by two large rosebushes. He looked around. To the left and right. Behind him. In front of him. Then he jammed his hand into the bush and snatched a fistful of roses, the thorns needling into his fingers and palm.

Hurt.

But he ran. He ran and ran, on and on. Left on Burman. Down Burman, left at Bryson's, which looked nothing like the houses on Portal Avenue. No big window. No shrubs or hedges. No driveway. A metal chain-linked fence that opened onto a walkway that led to the front door.

If Bryson hadn't paused the game to make himself a boloney sandwich, he wouldn't have heard the doorbell. He'd been playing *Call of Duty* all day, fighting against computerized versions of Nazis and doing everything he could, mission after mission, to not get himself killed along the way. His headset had been on since just after the morning oatmeal, his world of school rumors replaced by bombs in his ear. His hands were sore from yesterday, but that didn't stop him from thumbing the controller all day, even though his mother had warned him, told him it might be better if he'd read a book instead.

"Might be easier to hold a story than to hold a controller, son," she'd said, knowing Bryson wouldn't listen. "At least feed yourself," she'd added, giving up before closing his bedroom door and leaving for work.

And Bryson was doing just that, feeding himself—for the second time—when the doorbell rang.

Bryson shuffled his way over to the door, his body still feeling like garbled pixels. He looked through the peephole like his father taught him. Unlocked the dead bolt, turned the knob, pulled the door open.

"Ty?"

Ty stood there breathing heavy, holding three or four roses. It was hard to tell exactly how many because they were mangled. The human video game seemed to glitch in red streaks. The same red as the petals of the flowers was dripping from his shaking palm.

"You . . . okay, man?"

"Yeah," Ty wheezed, his back aching as if a school bus had fallen from the sky and landed right on him. "Yeah . . . I'm . . . okay. You okay?"

"Yeah, man. I'm fine. I'll . . . be fine."

Ty nodded. "Playing the game?" he asked, trying to figure out how to make it less awkward.

"Been fighting the war all day, bro." Bryson smirked, wiggling his thumbs. His eyes skipped from Ty's face to his shredded hand.

Ty nodded again. "Well . . . um . . . I brought these for you." He held the roses out.

"You ain't have to do that," Bryson said.

Ty nodded a third time. His eyes started to puff up and slick over. The rock in his throat began to roll. There were things they needed to talk about. Things they didn't need to talk about. There was a lot to say but nothing that needed to be said. Bryson carefully took the flowers. Smelled them like he'd seen his mother do. They made his nose itch.

"Hey, man, we'd better wash that blood off your hand," Bryson said, opening the door wide.

And Ty nodded once more.

CHESTNUT ST.

FIVE THINGS EASIER TO DO THAN SIMEON'S AND KENZI'S SECRET HANDSHAKE

1. Getting through the crowded hallway after the bell rings.

Simeon Cross was big for his age. Big, like two kids tall and two kids wide. A walking anvil with a happy gappy smile that lit every doorway he darkened. Impossible to miss when he was around and impossible not to miss when he was absent. So, when the bell rang, Simeon got up from his desk in Mr. Davanzo's class, grabbed his backpack off the floor, and waited by the door while all his classmates filed out, jumping up to give him high fives. Everybody but Ty Carson, who bolted out of class, probably because Mr. Davanzo couldn't stand people asking to go to the bathroom. "There's no time for breaks when it comes to understanding the world around you," he'd say.

After everyone else had gone, Simeon walked over to Mr. Davanzo, and they slapped the backs of their hands together, knuckles knocking like tiny pool balls. Their secret handshake. Which was nothing—elementary—compared to the complex system he and Kenzi had.

Kenzi Thompson was small for his age. Tied for the smallest kid in his class with another boy everybody called Bit. Kenzi didn't have a nickname like that, and if anyone ever tried to give him one, he would . . . do nothing. Well, that's not true. He would do something, but that something would be telling Simeon. And then Simeon would . . . do nothing. Because when you're Simeon's size, a look is more than enough.

Kenzi's name, though only five letters, was longer than he was. But other than his smallness—and the fact that he carried a blue bouncy ball everywhere he went—there was really nothing else about him that stood out. He wasn't particularly tough or loud or funny or sad or weird or even smelly. Just Kenzi. Maybe he'd speak in class. Maybe he wouldn't. Got good grades when he studied, bad grades when he didn't. Wasn't dripping in name brands, but always clean. And was friends with everyone. But really friends with no one but Simeon and Simeon was friends with everyone, because being his enemy just wasn't smart. Kenzi walked the middle of every line. Until the bell rang. And then . . . something else.

Kenzi never rushed out of Mr. Fantana's class like the rest of the students. Not because he had some kind of special love for life science—I mean, it was okay—but because he knew he'd never make it to his locker with the hundreds of other kids traffic-jamming and bumper-car'ing around, not paying attention to the fact that their elbows were right by his face. He'd been hit before. Several times. Had his eyes swollen accidentally by girls who swung their arms around to make sure their friends understood the importance of whatever they were saying. Had his lip busted because some boy was pretending it was five seconds left in the fourth quarter—*Curry with the ball, he shoots, he scores!*—and . . . he punches a kid in the face while hitting his crossover. That kid . . . Kenzi. For him, the hallway was a minefield, and there were hundreds of active mines dressed in T-shirts and jeans.

So he waited while Mr. Fantana gathered his lesson plans, put the tops back on his dry erase markers. Waited and waited. For . . .

"Yoooooooooooooooooo!" Simeon came bursting into Mr. Fantana's room. "Fantana Banana, what's good? What's hood? What's new? What's true?" Simeon gave Mr. Fantana an awkward handshake that looked like Mr. Fantana was trying to figure out how hands work.

"Took you forever, bro," Kenzi said, getting up from his desk.

"My bad, man," Simeon said, reaching out for Kenzi's hand.

"Don't!" Mr. Fantana sparked up. "*Don't* . . . don't do that handshake in here. Not because I think anything is wrong with it. It's just . . . I really want to get going, guys, and that handshake y'all do takes way too long. I know you probably won't believe this, but teachers have lives too." Mr. Fantana smirked, then went on shoving papers into his leather bag.

"*Wow* . . . Mr. Fantana I thought you were all about life science. What we were getting ready to show you was life science in full effect," Simeon explained.

"I am. And I love y'all, but . . . not today." Then he pointed at the door. "Please."

Simeon didn't argue. He just turned back to Kenzi.

"Come on, Kenzi. I don't wanna be nowhere we ain't welcomed."

"Simeon, cut it—" Mr. Fantana started, but Simeon shut him down.

"*Nope. Nope.* You said what you said, and the damage is done." Simeon bent his knees, squatting just enough for Kenzi to get a running start . . . to jump onto his back.

And off they went, out into the busy hallway of stumbling awkward bodies pin-balling around, bouncing into one another and off lockers. Simeon, bigger than the rest, was unbouncable. He couldn't be knocked down or pushed out of the way.

"Ready?" Simeon asked Kenzi over his shoulder. Kenzi had his arms wrapped around Simeon's neck, tight enough to hold on, but not tight enough to choke him.

"Let's do it!" Kenzi called back. And off they went.

2. Getting out of trouble with Ms. Wockley for pretending to be in a horse race.

"But, Ms. Wockley, we're not pretending to be in a horse race," Simeon pleaded. Ms. Wockley stood at the door to the school, her face a pink raisin, made raisinier whenever she was in discipline mode, which was all the time. It was pretty much her job to tell everyone what not to do.

Stop making fart noises.

Stop dancing.

Stop dancing . . . like that.

Stop rapping.

Stop singing.

Stop laughing.

Stop acting like children, children.

"Mr. Cross, Mr. Thompson was just on your back yelling *yee-haw* while circling his arm in the air as if winding an imaginary lasso." Ms. Wockley demonstrated, and it took everything in both boys to not crack up.

"That's just how he talks!" Simeon said.

"I'm going to say this to you for the thousandth time," Ms. Wockley steamed. "All feet should be—and stay firmly—on the ground."

"But what about Pia Foster? Her feet be on a skateboard." This, from Kenzi. It wasn't snitching because everybody knew Pia skated through school. The one time anyone had ever seen Simeon hurt was when Pia skated over his foot.

"And I've told her not to do that, but we're not talking about Ms. Foster, are we? No. We're talking about you two." Ms. Wockley folded her arms. "I've given you so many warnings, and you don't seem to take me seriously, so—"

"Wait, wait, wait. Before you write us up, I think it's important that we at least let you know why we do it."

Ms. Wockley sighed. She'd heard their excuse—different versions of it—time and time again, but they were always so entertaining that she was game to hear it once more.

"See, here's the thing, Wockley Broccoli. Can I call you that?" Simeon asked.

"No."

"Got it. Here's the thing. Kenzi here got a big heart. But that big heart happens to be in a small body. Now, I don't know about you, but I would hate for that heart to be broken because that body was knocked around. That would be a tragesty."

"Travesty," Kenzi corrected him.

"Travesty," Simeon repeated. "And so because I love Kenzi, I protect him. I make sure he can maneuver down these busy hallways without worrying about anything. I'm basically his bodyguard."

"Tell me something, Mr. Cross. How exactly does Mr. Thompson get from class to class during the day when he's not with you?" Simeon knew this was a setup.

"I know where you going with this, and I don't know because I'm not with him, Ms. Wockley. But I can only *imagine* how scary it must be." Simeon put his arm around Kenzi. Kenzi turned his face into a puppy's.

"Is that true, Mr. Thompson, that the hallways are scary for you?"

"Oh, Ms. Wockley, you got no idea. Just the other day Joey Santiago didn't see me standing behind him and just backed me into my locker."

"Like . . . backed him all the way into it. As in his whole body was in—"

"I understand what he's saying, Mr. Cross. He has a mouth."

"Exactly, he does have a mouth." Simeon was right there with her. "He also has arms and legs. Feet and hands. And in the same way you don't want him silenced, you also don't want him invisible, do you?"

"Yeah, you don't want me to be invisible, do you, Ms. Wockley?"

Ms. Wockley's tight face was still tight, but a little less tight than it was when Kenzi and Simeon had gotten caught—pulled over—by her.

"If I could just make one more point, Ms. Wockley—"

She cut Simeon off. "You can't. Please just go home and come back tomorrow ready to follow the rules." Ms. Wockley marched off, the sound of her chunky heels clacking loudly. She turned and added, "When you two grow up, I really hope you become more than horse and jockey, because people lose *a lot* of money betting on horse races."

"Not if they bet on us," Simeon zapped right back at her.

"Plus, I want to be a lawyer," Kenzi said, trying to control the sting in his throat. "Because they're smart and they know stuff like . . . jockeys don't say *yee-haw*. Cowboys do."

3. Getting to the neighborhood.

Outside was what outside always was—a spill-out of inside. It was like the main hallway was the river that led into the ocean of backpacks, ball caps, and braids. Energy and engines roaring the roar of *school is finally over*.

"Yo, you got old Wocka Wocka outta here with that cowboy line. Plus, I ain't no horse. I'm a friend. Your brother," Simeon said to Kenzi as they walked up to the corner. Ms. Post, the crossing guard, was standing there with her arms out.

"Hey, boys," she said. Kenzi leaned in for a hug.

"Hey, Ms. Post." That hug happened every day between Kenzi and the crossing guard. A walking ritual.

"Staying out of trouble?" she asked.

"Of course," Simeon said. "Matter of fact, I'm going home to do my homework. Because we have homework. Not sure Canton here told you this or not, but there's homework."

Canton was Ms. Post's son. He was sitting leaning against the stop sign on the corner waiting for her, like he did every day. Canton just shook his head, paying the big guy no mind because everyone was used to him being silly.

"And what about you, little man?" Ms. Post addressed Kenzi. "Staying out the street?"

"Trying," Kenzi followed, holding the blue ball up, as if she could look into it and see the day's behavior.

"What about *you*?" Simeon now asked Ms. Post, who had put a hand up to signal for other walkers to hold tight on the corner and wait for her whistle.

"Best I can," she replied, popping the silver tweeter in her mouth and stepping back off the curb.

"Catch you tomorrow, Ms. Post," Kenzi said, waving as he and Simeon turned right. Most walkers walked to the left down Portal Avenue toward some of the other neighborhoods, but to the right—up Portal *Ave.*—is where Chestnut Homes were. Where Simeon and Kenzi lived. It took no time, because there were very few of their classmates going that way. And the ones who actually lived there didn't walk there. So the path was clear, laid out for Simeon the Grand and Kenzi the Great, like a runway to their kingdom. A kingdom where carrying a person on your back was allowed. Encouraged, even. A kingdom where kings are throned and dethroned daily. Where the crown jewels get dropped down sewers and flushed down toilets. A kingdom full of princes, like Kenzi and Simeon, princes no one ever bet on anyway.

"Anyway, like I was saying. We family." Simeon nailed down what he was going on about before they stopped to talk to Ms. Post.

"Exactly. You my brother," Kenzi confirmed, bouncing the blue ball as they approached Chestnut Street.

The way Kenzi and Simeon thought about it, Chestnut Street is a paradise. Light poles are like palm trees, bus stop benches like hammocks, and corner stores like island bungalows.

There's a smell in the air. A mix of exhaust and exhaustion. Also cooked food and cooked hair.

There's a feel in the air. A stickiness like walking through an invisible syrup. A thickness to life.

There's a sound in the air. A shrill and chill. The

scream and whisper of the world making a symphony of *so good* and *so what*. Also, the sound of Kenzi and Simeon, their voices still young, still sweet like flutes cutting through.

Most people tighten up when they walk down Chestnut. Tuck tails and tuck chains. But for Kenzi and Simeon, this was where they could let loose. Where they could run and slap the street signs pretending to dunk. Where they could stand on the blue mailboxes like pedestals or see who could balance the longest on the tip-top of a fire hydrant. Where they could open random doors of random shops and speak to the owners—Mrs. Wilson's beauty supply store (Tell your mama I got new wigs!) or Mr. Chase's hardware store (Your daddy get the sink to stop leaking yet?) or Sue, who owned the Chinese restaurant and was always too busy to speak to them. But nowhere was better than Fredo's.

4. Picking the perfect snack from Fredo's Corner Store.

Walking into Fredo's was like walking into a dungeon, no matter what time of day it was. The light was always dim, and the shelves were packed so high that you couldn't see over them. Walls of whatnot. No windows. Big enough for the world's snacks, but too small for anything else. Always smelled like incense smoke trying to mask dirty mop water.

Kenzi and Simeon came through the door with the kind of confidence of someone who owned the place.

"Fredo!" Simeon called out, throwing up a hand, while heading toward the Bundt cakes and boxes of mini doughnuts.

"Well, if isn't Wreck-It-Ralph and Tiny Tim," Fredo shot back. He was flipping through the newspaper, licking his fingers every few seconds to turn the pages, as if anyone could read that fast. "You know, I look through this paper every day, hoping I don't see y'all faces."

"You never will," Kenzi said. "Unless it's for something good."

"Something good like what?" Fredo asked, setting the paper on the counter.

"Something good like me becoming a big-time lawyer," Kenzi replied.

"Yeah, or like me becoming a famous actor," Simeon said. "So I can *act* like a big-time lawyer." He picked up a snack cake, turned it over to check the expiration date. No telling how long Fredo kept things, and they'd bought cakes that tasted like bricks before.

"Listen, it's more likely a school bus will fall from the sky."

"Ouch." Simeon gripped his chest dramatically.

"Don't get me wrong. I hope all that happens so y'all can buy this store and I can retire, kick back and watch *Law and Order* marathons all day, every day."

"Well, we'd have to change the name of this place," Simeon said, accidentally bumping bags of chips off the shelves behind him. "To something like K&S Food."

"Or S&K food," Kenzi suggested.

Fredo knitted his fingers together, rested his hands on the counter like some kind of judge. "Okay, gentlemen. Whatever you say."

A few moments later Kenzi and Simeon were at the counter. A bag of chips for Kenzi. And a snack cake for Simeon. A MoonPie.

"Fifty cents each, boys," Fredo said.

"I got you," Simeon said to Kenzi, sliding Kenzi's chips over to be included with his cake.

"Okay, so that's gonna be a dollar, big man."

And then came the change. Simeon reached into his pocket and pulled out a fistful of dimes and nickels and pennies, slapped them down on the counter and started separating them and counting them out as if he were setting a checkers board. Kenzi chuckled. He was used to Simeon doing stuff like this, and seeing all that change on the counter, he couldn't help but think about how Bit Burns—Kenzi's short twin in school—who had a reputation for patting people's pockets and stealing their change would never try that on Simeon.

"Hold on, let me count it out," Simeon said. "Five. Ten. Fifteen. Sixteen. Seventeen. Twenty-seven. Twenty-eight . . ."

"How your brother?" Fredo asked Simeon.

"He a'ight. Probably somewhere in the street, driving that old ice-cream truck around, frontin' like he legit."

Fredo nodded, then nodded at Kenzi. "And what about yours? I see you still carrying that old handball of his everywhere you go. You know he ain't no good at that game, right?" And before Kenzi could answer, Simeon got frustrated and slammed his hand on the counter.

"You made me lose count, man!" Simeon boomed. "*Gah!* Now I gotta start all over. Five. Ten. Fif—"

"*Okay*," Fredo said, scooping the right amount off the counter and into his palm. "We'll be here all day."

"Where you gotta go, Fredo?" Simeon taunted.

"To your mother's house. Ask her how many times she dropped you when you were a baby."

"Oh, no need to ask her that. I can tell you. She only dropped me once, into a vat of gold."

"And a vat of gravy," Fredo cracked, but Simeon didn't laugh. And because Simeon didn't laugh, Kenzi stepped up.

"Better chill, Fredo," Kenzi warned. "Matter of fact, just for that . . ." And then, up on his tippy-toes, he reached over and grabbed Fredo's newspaper off the counter. And when Fredo didn't budge, Kenzi snatched his lighter, too. This got Fredo's attention. "No more cigarettes. They bad for you anyway."

"No more of them booty-funk incense either," Simeon said, opening the door, his laughter lingering in the store after he and Kenzi left. Such silly things to take, a gossipy newspaper and a lighter, as if Fredo ain't own a store. One with a bunch of newspapers and matches and lighters behind the counter. But still, it was about the principle. The loyalty. The brotherhood.

5. Making wishes.

When Kenzi and Simeon made it to their building, the building they'd been living in their entire lives, they sat out front on the steps. The whole walk home they laughed about Fredo, making up silly jokes about him.

"Fredo look like a puppet, like somebody got their hand up his butt controlling him," Kenzi snapped.

"He look like the type of dude who would own a store that just sells . . . snacks. Like, you know what kind of guy you gotta be to just sell snacks? *Snacks?*" From Simeon, who now had the newspaper and rolled it up into a tube. He swung it around like a short sword.

"What do Fredo even mean? I mean, if it's *Al*fredo, that would explain it, because he definitely cheesy," Kenzi piled on, bouncing his ball back and forth under his legs. A slight breeze blew litter around. Plastic bags floating like jellyfish, and a deflated birthday balloon—

one of the shiny metallic ones—lifted and zipped through the air like happy shrapnel.

"Exactly. Cheesy. But I can't front, he got me with the gravy joke." Simeon followed the balloon with his eyes as if it were a football thrown long. Or a messenger pigeon with a note from afar. A smirk crept onto his face.

"Yeah he did," Kenzi agreed, and they both cracked up. Kenzi set the ball down, opened his bag of chips, offered Simeon some.

"Nah, I'm good," Simeon said as the balloon floated out of view. "But . . . gimme that lighter." Kenzi handed Simeon Fredo's lighter, unsure of what he was going to do with it. He couldn't grow up to be a lawyer if Simeon was getting ready to set something on fire. Jokes were one thing, but burning stuff down was something totally different. Simeon unrolled the newspaper; glanced at the front page, which was a story about a school bus falling from the sky; and ripped it in half. Then ripped the half in half and twisted it into a paper worm. At least that's what it looked like. Then he took the MoonPie from its plastic, his huge fingers crushing most of it trying to slide it out perfectly.

"Happy Birthday to you," Simeon started singing in a fake opera voice. *"Happy Birthday to you."*

"What?"

"Happy Birthday, dear Kenziiiii. Happy Birthdayyyyyyy,

to . . . *youuuuuuuUuUuuuUUUUuuu.*" Simeon stuck the paper worm into the MoonPie, making it a wick. Then he lit the end of it on fire.

"Happy Birthday, my man. I would've sang you the Black people version, but I ain't want to turn this special moment into a concert," Simeon said, holding the MoonPie out for Kenzi. The growing flame licked the air.

"It's . . . not my birthday, bro."

"Quick, quick, blow it out before it turns this Moon-Pie to a s'more."

Kenzi gave in, leaned over.

"And don't forget to make a wish!"

Kenzi thought for a moment, then huffed the fire out, bits of scorched paper flying off like black snowflakes. The smoke corkscrewing up into the air.

"What you wish for?" Simeon asked.

"I ain't telling you because then it won't come true."

"*True*," Simeon said, standing up. "Well, since I can't know your wish, I might as well go get at this homework. Mr. Davanzo wants us to write about environmental something. I don't know, but I know I'll get a better view looking out my apartment window. You can see more from up there." Simeon pulled the paper out of the MoonPie. He split the snack, stuffed half in his mouth and gave the other half to Kenzi.

"Yeah, I'm out too," Kenzi said, back on his feet as well. He shoved his half of the MoonPie in his mouth too. Slipped the ball in his bag. Had to free his hands for what was coming.

The handshake:

They grab hands, shake, shake, slide, finger grip, shake, shake.

Then point to themselves, double fist bump, throw a peace sign beside each of their right ears, point to each other, slap their individual fingertips together, rub the air as if they were holding a ball—bigger than the one in Kenzi's bag—then they thumb their chins and shake their heads at each other before ending it with a big hug.

"Brothers," Simeon said.

"Brothers," Kenzi repeated, his voice muffled by the MoonPie he was still chewing.

They did it just like they'd watched their older brothers do it. The same shake. The same secret. The same bond. On the same steps. And as they rode the elevator up to their separate floors—Simeon on seven, Kenzi on nine—Simeon looked at Kenzi, knowing what he wished for. And Kenzi looked at Simeon, knowing Simeon knew that he wished the smoke from the paper candle could drift, could carry a note through the air, across the city and state, over lands and highways he'd never been on, through barbed wire, stone, and iron, ghosting its way through bars and into the ear of his brother.

To tell him how he wished he didn't have to walk home from school.

How he wished his brother, Mason, could pick him up in a car just like the car Simeon's brother, Chucky, had stolen almost two years ago. The one Mason took the hit for, went down for.

But not that one.

A different one.

And took Kenzi for a ride.

Maybe even showed him how to play.

SATCHMO'S
MASTER
PLAN

TODAY, AFTER school, Satchmo Jenkins worked out a master plan to save his life.

A plan he wished he'd come up with a long time ago.

It started back when Satchmo was bit. He was seven years old and the rottweiler was thirty-two years old, which was old enough for him to know better, Satchmo had thought. The dog had taken a chunk out of the back of Satchmo's leg, left teeth marks that scarred in the shape of a sad face. It was a freak accident, a moment that no one could've predicted because Satchmo Jenkins never ever missed. Whenever a ball was thrown toward him, he was sure to snatch it from the air. He was known for this. But when Clancy had told him to go long and heaved the football into the air, Satchmo had tried his best to extend his body, stretched out for it, but it was just beyond him. Overthrown. And when the ball hit the ground, it took the worst possible bounce right into Ms. Adams's yard, where Brutus the Rottweiler lived, chained to a tree. When the ball tumbled Brutus's way, he jumped up, tail like a stubby index finger wagging hard enough to knock him off-balance, nosed the ball and tried to get his mouth around it, tried to get his teeth locked down on the pigskin. But Brutus's excitement got the best of him, and he ended up knocking the ball just past the length of the chain restraining him. Perfect for Satchmo.

"Yo, Satch," Clancy had called. "Hurry up and get it before Ms. Adams sees you."

Ms. Adams was Brutus's owner. An older lady who sat in the window and watched the neighborhood, making sure no one stepped foot in her yard, as if her grass was a different kind of grass, like she had it flown in from wherever mean people get grass from. Sometimes she'd have the window wide open, even when it was freezing cold, and she'd just be sitting there, looking, the bottom of her mouth sagging from the tobacco she always had stuffed down in her lip. Sometimes she'd spit black juice loogies halfway across the yard. Clean pellet-size ones, like shooting bullets out of her mouth. Other times she'd spit in a jar. The rumor was she'd mix that tobacco slime with Brutus's food. Make him extra mean. Make sure anyone that came into her yard knew they were dealing with a beast who could only be held by a big bull chain wrapped around a fat-trunked tree. And when she saw Satchmo, instead of doing the old lady wave and *Hey, how's your mother*, like some of the other grown-ups in the neighborhood, Ms. Adams just nodded slightly.

Satchmo had always imagined the inside of her house was like an old boxing gym. That it was bare and cold and smoky, heavy bags hanging from the ceiling that Ms. Adams gave bare-knuckle jabs and right hooks to. Maybe she even kicked them. Kneed them. Some elbows. Sometimes Satchmo even thought that maybe he had it all wrong, that maybe Brutus wasn't Ms. Adam's guard dog, but instead, she was Brutus's guard lady. She was there to protect the dog. To bite anyone who tried to get close to him with those black-stained teeth.

Satchmo had looked to see if Ms. Adams was sitting in the window. Then glanced back at Clancy, who shook his head no, as in, *No, she ain't there.* As in, *Yes, you should do this.* As in, *Hurry up.* So Satchmo tipped off the street and onto the sidewalk, then off the sidewalk and into the yard of Brutus Adams, a basketball-headed rottweiler, black, with a heart of brown around his mouth.

"Hey there, Brutus," Satchmo whispered, creeping

toward the football. There was nothing to fear, because the ball was far enough away from the dog that there was no way Brutus could get to him. But with each step, Brutus's tail would wag harder and harder. Wagging like *yes, yes, yes,* and *no, no, no* at the same time. Wagging like *I'm happy to see you, and I want to play, but we play different games. You never miss. Me either.* Wagging like . . .

Satchmo picked up the ball. Wiped the slobber on his jeans.

. . . finders keepers . . .

He held the ball up, a sign of victory for Clancy to see. Clancy put his hands in the air as if Satchmo had just retrieved a fumble. Victory.

Wag. Wag. Wag, wag, wag, wag. Panting. Jumping. Jumping. Barking.

. . . losers . . . runners!

Satchmo glanced over his shoulder, and Brutus, now more excited than ever, was charging toward him, the chain snatching him back, but only for a second before he tried again, lifting up on his hind legs and towering over Satchmo, who had now started running back toward the street.

But it was too late. The game had already begun. And seconds later the chain snapped, and Brutus came blasting toward Satchmo.

Satchmo was named after Louis Armstrong, a

famous jazz musician his grandmother loved. The story goes that Louis was nicknamed Satchmo because he had such a big mouth, a "satchel mouth." However, Satchmo Jenkins's mouth wasn't big at all, but he learned that day that it could be a trumpet if he needed it to. It could screech and honk and run up and down a scale as long as there was a dog making him run up and down a street.

Four years later, Satchmo moved from his old neighborhood to Marlow Hill, after his mother had taken a job as an office assistant at a veterinary clinic. Satchmo's run-in with Brutus had sparked a new dream of being a vet, and though she'd have to go through years of school and training to make that happen, she looked at this job, this move, as a step in the right direction. And now that she worked close to animals, she made sure Satchmo knew how to handle himself around dogs. But no matter what his mother said, no matter what she taught him, it didn't matter. Fear had clamped down on his brain and the scars on the back of his leg—the raised dots and dashes like Morse code on his skin—served as a reminder that dogs were dangerous.

He'd heard people say, "If they got teeth, they'll bite," and he watched his mother push back and argue against that, and on the flip side he'd seen all the commercials of sad pups locked behind cages, sick and shivering, and the voice of some celebrity trying to convince people to adopt one. And he'd say, some-times out loud, "Maybe they're in there for a reason." His mother didn't like that either.

"Your bite was a misunderstanding, Satch," she'd say. "He wanted to play, but you got tense, so then he got tense because your tension made it clear to him that you weren't playing."

"Why would I want to play when he was barking and growling? His *play-play* looked like *bite-bite*."

But small dogs didn't bother him. As long as they were no bigger than a football, he could deal. Anything bigger caused his back to tighten. Made his heart bark. Thankfully, since living in Marlow Hill, his walks home had been dogless.

Until yesterday.

Yesterday, he was walking down Nestle Street when he passed Mr. Jerry's house and saw something out of the corner of his eye. Something big. And furry. It darted across the patch of grass Mr. Jerry had along the side of his house, blocked off by a chain-link fence.

Satchmo's stomach dropped to his feet, his throat twisted like twines making rope. He turned his head to see what he knew he'd already seen. To make sure that his first thought—and peripheral vision—hadn't lied. Mr. Jerry had gotten a dog.

Mr. Jerry's wife had passed away a few months ago. A week later, Satchmo stood with his mother at Mr. Jerry's front door, a house plant in his hand. His mother was holding a pound cake she'd made him as a way to say *Sorry for your loss*. And Satchmo wished the pound cake was enough and that his mother didn't have to keep talking and suggest Mr. Jerry get a dog. Adopt one from a shelter.

Pound cake. *Not a dog from the pound*, Satchmo thought.

"Lose a life, save another," his mother said to Mr. Jerry sweetly.

To take mine, Satchmo had thought.

Mr. Jerry said *no, no, no*. Said he wasn't ready. Guess he was ready now. And not for a small one. Not for a furry football. But for a big, husky thing that looked like it was mixed. Some German shepherd. Some Labrador. Some rottweiler, some monster that Satchmo wasn't sure was there or not, but decided it was so.

That was all he needed to see to start devising plans. Escape routes.

Today, after school, Satchmo Jenkins left his last class of the day, math, and headed to his locker in a haze. He opened it, swapped out books and stuck his head in his locker for a moment to take a few deep breaths to get himself together. This walk home was going to be a big one. One that he hoped wouldn't result in him adding a smiley-faced scar on his other leg.

"Satch, catch," John John Watson called out, tossing a textbook at Satchmo, who looked up at just the right time to not be hit in the face. He blocked the book with his hands, then tried to grab ahold—tried to catch it—fumbling, fumbling, fumbling it before it hit the floor. "You left it in Mrs. Stevens's class," John John said. He pulled a few random sandwich bags from his pocket, folded them awkwardly, then stuffed them back down.

"Oh. Good looks," Satchmo said, trying to snap himself out of it or at least pretend he was never snapped into it. "Lifesaver."

"No problem," John John said, before hustling off.

Satchmo picked the book up, tossed it in the air, caught it. A small piece of paper slid out from between the pages—an invitation to Cynthia Sower's comedy show. But Satchmo was in no mood for laughing. He tossed the book in the air again, caught it again, before putting it in his bag and closing the locker door. Snap.

After he got outside, headed toward the corner, made the right on Portal as if walking toward Chestnut Street, but making the right onto Nestle before getting to Chestnut, he started running down his game plan, amping himself up for the mission. That's what this was for him—a mission.

Okay, Satch. You're prepared.

You've thought it all through.

You will not get bit. You will not get eaten.

Breathe, Satch. Breathe   and work it
all out.
  If the dog jumps the fence,
  when *the dog jumps the fence   don't panic.*
  Just do what you've planned.
  Break to the right.   If Mr. Jerry's pickup truck is
          parked on the street, jump into
the   *back of it and*
  scream   *for help.*
  That's the first base. That's your go-to. But
          if for some reason Mr. Jerry's truck isn't there,
                  if for some reason he's out, I don't know,
saving   *other dogs while his neighbors run for their lives,*
  then keep going right onto the Carters' property.
  You won't have time to ring their doorbell,
    plus Mr. and Mrs. Carter will be at work,
  so run
  behind their house. They have a pool. It's not a big pool,
  and actually you've never even seen it, but you remember
  your mother talking about
  how all the neighbors are gossiping about how they were
  putting a pool in their backyard
      in this neighborhood,
  and she was saying it like she wasn't gossiping too,
  so if there's actually a pool back there   dive in.
  Don't worry about how deep it is.
  You can swim.

Just jump in there. Hopefully the dog won't even follow
you back there, but if
it does, maybe it won't jump in the pool. But if
for some reason
it does jump in, you jump out.
> *Immediately.*
The thing is, dogs have to do that ridiculous
> *doggy paddle thing,*
so they can't be vicious and do that at the same time.
They also can't do that fast.   They're dogs, not seals.
So when you hop out, you'll have a head start
before the dog gets to the other side of the pool
> *and climbs back onto land. Use this*
time to jump the fence
your mother says the Carters put up to keep Ms. Winston's
> *little kids*
from playing in their pool that we're not sure exists.
But the fence is there. You know that. It's not too high,
but get a running start because you're going to be
soaking wet. If you still can't get over, then quickly
as quickly as possible take off your
shirt and pants and shoes, and
try again. Sure, you need your clothes, but you need your
> *life more.*
Your mother will understand, and you'll get over the
> *embarrassment*
of being outside in your underwear.

Once you're over the fence you should be safe,
    because the dog should be too tired
from all the swimming to jump the fence. But it's going to
try. And while it's trying you better be booking it back
to the street, and home. But   if for some reason,
    when you get back
to the street, the dog is there waiting for you man
            you might be dead.
No. No, no, no.
If for some reason the dog is there waiting for you,
    break off and jump
on that old car that's been sitting in front of
    Sadani's house. After Sadani
had his car stolen a few years ago, he only ever buys old
    crappy cars
that he can't get working, so he won't mind you jumping on
the hood. And if the dog jumps on
the hood with you, climb to the roof. The dog should slip
on the windshield some, but don't count on that.
    While he's slipping
        and sliding,
jump off the car and see if it's unlocked. Sadani never
    locks the doors
of those cars because he knows
they're impossible to start and
therefore impossible to steal.
If it's open, jump in, close the door.

This is a safe place
because you don't need to turn the car on
    to roll the windows down.
It will have the old kind of window roll-downer.
    Crack the window and scream until help comes.
But   if for some reason the door is locked, pull the
sausage patties you saved from this morning's breakfast out
    and
fling them like Frisbees. If the dog doesn't go for them
though really, who wouldn't? then you'll have to
    break out your routes.
    Your zigs and zags.
Just like back when you and Clancy pretended to be in
    the Super Bowl,
him the quarterback and
you the wide receiver.
Where do you think Clancy is?
What do you think he's doing right now?
    Throwing Hail Marys?
    Running the opposite way?
    Not helping his teammates?
Why didn't he chase Brutus?
Why didn't he tackle him?
If he would've tackled him, you would've barked at it.
Growled at it so it knew what that felt like.
    Not important right now. What's important
is making sure you have your

zigs and zags ready. Be prepared to cut
left and cut right,
stutter and juke,
stagger and jerk.
He has four legs and you have two, there's no way
the dog will be able to keep up, right?
Or maybe the more legs the better?
Who knows, but do it anyway.
Zig and zag   all the way home.
When you get to your house, run around
to the side door that you left unlocked
this morning knowing your mother would kill you
if she knew you left the door unlocked
because y'all don't have a guard dog
or an alarm system.
If for some reason, some strange reason, that side door
is locked   well, Satchmo
you'll have to just pray
for a miracle.   A distraction. Something crazy
like a school bus falling from the sky.

This is what Satchmo told himself, what he was
ready to execute—the master plan to save his life—as
he approached Mr. Jerry's house. Satchmo had purposely walked on the other side of the street to give
himself a little bit of an advantage. No need to bait the
beast. As he slinked past Mr. Jerry's front door, coming up on his side yard, Satchmo's backbone became

rawhide, his stomach a squishy chew toy, his palms wet but his fingers dry like dog treats, when he heard the bark. Well, not really a bark, but the gruff voice of an old man.

"Satch! Satch!"

Mr. Jerry was calling out for him. He was kneeling behind the fence, rubbing the dog's head, its tongue slapping the old man's cheek. No bite-bite.

Love-love.

"Satch, come here," Mr. Jerry said, his face a touchdown dance all its own. "I want to introduce you to my friend."

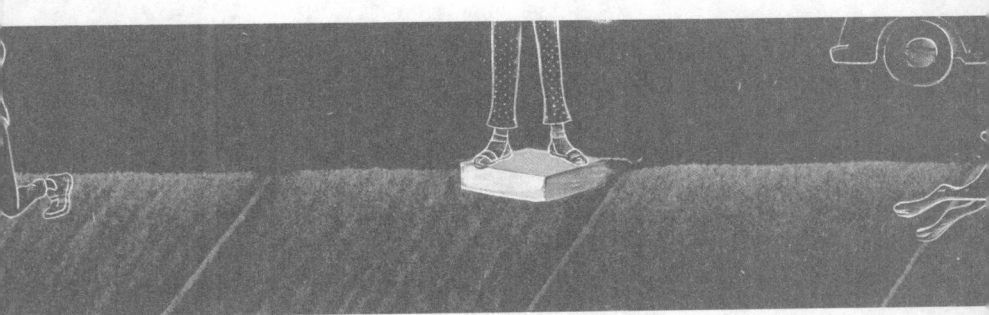

SOUTHVIEW AVE.

OOKABOOKA LAND

"GATHER, GATHER, gather round, ladies and gentlemen, leopards and giraffes, lollipops and gummy bears, lizard lips and googly-eyes, and yes, even you . . . Mrs. Stevens. I am the super-super Say-So, and I've come to make you laugh until you pass. Pass what, you ask? Pass gas. Pass out. Pass away. Pass anything other than . . . class."

"Careful," Mrs. Stevens warned from her desk in the corner of the room. She sat with her arms folded, watching Cynthia "Say-So" Sower put on a show in front of the class. This was the only way to keep Cynthia from disrupting and derailing the entire lesson. If Mrs. Stevens didn't give her these five minutes at the end, Cynthia would burst into some kind of sideways monologue about whatever Mrs. Stevens had been teaching that day. Like how negative numbers deserve empathy because no one should ever feel lower than zero.

"I mean, wouldn't you feel a little negative too, if people kept saying you less than nothing? You basically don't even really exist. You under under. Your mama done probably kicked you out. Your girlfriend or boyfriend done broke up with you, and when you asked why, they just said something like, you ain't enough for me. So tell me, who is crying for the negative number? Who, Mrs. Stevens? *Whoooo?*" Cynthia would wail and flail overdramatic fists in the air, all leading up to the big finish, Cynthia planting her face flat on the desk. Cheek to wood. And right when Mrs. Stevens would think it was over, Cynthia would lift up and ask, "You know what I would do if I was a negative number?"

There was only one answer.

"Cynthia, don't you dare," Mrs. Stevens warned, knowing what was coming.

There was always only one answer.

"I . . . would . . ."

One answer, and the whole class knew it.

"Cynthia. Seriously." Mrs. Stevens shook her head.

And because the whole class knew it, they joined in and said it with her.

"*RUN!*"

Cynthia would jump up from her desk and charge

out of the classroom. But only for a second. Then she'd come back in as if it never happened, have a seat at her desk, straighten her posture, pick up her pencil with one hand, and play with the two plaits sprouting from either side of her head—a hairstyle she loved for its comedic effect—with the other. Mrs. Stevens used to call out for her, used to stutter-step toward the door, used to threaten to write her up.

"Don't *divide* me from the class, Mrs. Stevens. *Please.* Don't . . . *divide* us!" Cynthia would fake beg, doubling down on the math joke.

"Oh, I'm not planning on doing any division, Cynthia. I'm thinking more along the lines of subtraction."

But Mrs. Stevens never did. Truth is, she liked Cynthia's jokes. It reminded her of old comedians on the black-and-white TV shows her grandmother used to watch when she was a child. So she cut the goofball a deal. If Cynthia could be attentive and serious all class, she would get the last five minutes to do her thing.

"So, L's and G's, let's start with the news. This just in: Shirt . . . is a strange word, right? I mean, seriously, there had to be better options when it came to naming . . . this." Cynthia tugged at the collar of her T-shirt. "I heard—and this is just what I *heard*—a long, long, long time ago, there was this dude who was a clothes maker, and he invented this thing to cover your chest and arms and stuff. Now, when he first made it, he called it an arm-belly-chest cloth. But that name was too long, so then he shortened it to an ABC. But then, the ABCs came out and y'know *that* became a whole thing with the song, and the cool *LMNOP* part, and the next thing he knew, everybody was doing it, and the clothes maker realized maybe ABC wasn't the best name to call his arm-belly-chest cloth. But he ain't have another name for it. One night, he was sitting with a friend. No, not one friend, a bunch of his friends. At a dinner. And everybody's trying on his arm-belly-chest cloth thing, right? And the clothes maker is nervous, because people love it and they keep asking him what it's called. And when he tells them, their faces drop, like they can't believe it. 'That's too long of a name. We call shoes, shoes. Not toe cover-uppers!' they said. Now, see, the clothes maker was a nervous eater. I forgot to tell y'all that part. Every time he got stressed out or, like, anxious, he would eat. And now he was nervous because everyone was saying his garment wouldn't work unless he changed the name. 'So what are you going to change it to?' they asked. And instead of responding, he just started stuffing bread in his mouth. Bread, bread, bread. Just pushing it in there. 'What are you going to name it?' they repeated. And do you know what the clothes maker said with a mouth full of rolls?" Pause, for effect. "I'll tell you what he said," Cynthia wound up. "The clothes maker shrugged and said all muffled, '*Shirt*, I don't know!'"

And before the ruckus could even come, Mrs. Stevens shut it all down.

"*Okay*. Okay . . . that's enough for today!" she said, trying not to laugh herself. There was no need to cut Cynthia off anyway, because the punchline landed at the exact moment the bell rang.

Cynthia's mother worked all day and went to school all evening, and when Cynthia was a baby, her mother would rock her to sleep with bedtime stories read out of night school textbooks. She was Cynthia's hero. A hero too busy to save her. A hero too hardworking to even find time to laugh. But a hero nonetheless. But Cynthia's grandfather was her superhero. Not in the superhuman sense, but in the way that there was something incredible about him. At least to Cynthia. To almost everyone else, he was just the wild ex-soldier who owned the liquor store right in front of her apartment building. The kind of man who would take a wooden crate, flip it upside down, then step up on it and put on a show. Hold court right there in the middle of the store. Jokes were his superpower. The dirtier the better. Cynthia was even named after him.

His name was Cinder. And whenever he'd introduce himself to people, they'd always ask, "Cinder, like Cinderella?"

And he'd say, "Nah. Cinder, like cinder block."

But really, he was a bit of both. Had a toughness to him. A hardheaded, hardhanded, hard-talking man. But he was also soft. Soft enough to hold baby Cynthia and stare at her and laugh and laugh like she was the greatest joke ever told. Soft enough to know a good sidekick when he saw one. Soft enough to give her a nickname. Sweetie Say-So. Named her that because of all the goo-goos, gah-gahs, and grunts Cynthia would make whenever Cinder would pick her up. A noisemaker. Always a noisemaker. And Cinder would just salute her and say, "Sweetie, if you say so. If you say so, sweetie."

Cinder's girlfriend—a gray-haired, lipsticked, cigarette-smoking mail woman named Miss Fran—would always come by his store to deliver letters and bills, always catching him in the middle of his jokester routines. She'd laugh in this way that made all the bottles in the store rattle. Made all the men jealous of the love thing she and Cinder had. And when she came on Saturdays, she'd always catch Cynthia marching around outside the front of the store—prompted by her grandfather—and Miss Fran would stick stamps on Cynthia's chubby cheeks and forehead.

"I'm gon' put you in the mailbox. Ship you off to Ookabooka Land," she'd tease, and Cynthia would laugh and scream *no*, as if Ookabooka Land were a real place.

Miss Fran died when Cynthia was seven. Hurt Cynthia

to lose the only grandmother she'd ever known, but her sadness was nothing compared to Cinder's. Seemed like Cinder's mind floated away with Miss Fran's spirit and voice. Or maybe it went underground with her body, buried in the cemetery across the street from the liquor store. Cinder could see her gravestone from the window of the fourth-floor unit he and Miss Fran had lived in together, five doors down from where Cynthia lived with her mom.

It wasn't long after Miss Fran's death that Cinder closed the liquor store. It wasn't long after the store closed that it was knocked down. It wasn't long after it was knocked down that the apartment complex built a playground where it used to be. A sliding board. A set of swings. A seesaw. A stage. Not a big, elaborate stage, just a concrete platform about the size of the wooden crates Cinder used to stand on in the store, a bronze plaque bolted to it that read, **CINDER'S BLOCK**. Cynthia hoped that maybe he'd step up on it someday. Crack a joke or two. But he never would because it wasn't long after the store was turned into a playground that Cinder started to forget things. How to turn on the radio. How to work the microwave. And every time something simple would slip his mind, Cynthia would have to come over to help.

"Remind me how to turn on the TV, Say-So. Don't seem to wanna work for me," Cinder would say, pointing the case he kept his eyeglasses in at the television screen.

Wasn't long after Cinder started to forget things that Cynthia and her mother moved down the hall into her grandfather's two-bedroom apartment. Cinder had his room. And Cynthia and her mother had the other, which meant, most nights, because her always-exhausted mother slept like a woman fighting a bear, Cynthia slept on the couch dreaming of the day she could make her mother laugh. Dreaming of the day she could funny her mother free of all the work, of all the stress she seemed to wear on her face like thick makeup the wrong color for her skin. Dreaming of her mother telling her a joke. *Knock knock.* And Cynthia replying, *Who's there?* And her mother saying, *Me.* And Cynthia *not* having to say *Me, who?*

That's all Say-So ever wanted. A love thing with her mother, the way her grandfather had with Miss Fran—through laughter. And since her mother was too busy to break, well then, anyone would have to do. A smile is a smile. A *ha* is a *ha*. So every day she'd rattle off her jokes at the end of class, bathing in her classmates' crack-ups.

Including today.

As everyone rushed out of Mrs. Stevens's class, Cynthia stood at the door handing out flyers. Not the kind that are professionally printed with graphics and lasers and cool shadow effects. These were just pieces of lined notebook paper, ripped into squares (with soggy edges because she believed in the lick and rip method) that said, written in red, **SAY-SO LIVE ON CINDER'S BLOCK AT THE SOUTHVIEW APARTMENTS. SHOW STARTS AT 3:33.**

"Be there or be . . . Mr. Fantana's forever-wedgie," Cynthia teased. She didn't know where that one came from, but she let it loose and let it live.

Down the hall she went, stopping at her locker, grabbing her things, and heading for the door, pausing only to tell her friend Gregory Pitts that he smells like his last name. She told him this every day just because . . . just because. And Greg, knowing it was a joke, flapped his arms like a bird, wafting the pit funk toward her.

"Three thirty-three!" she called out to him. "Be there."

When she got outside, instead of taking the long way she usually took and walking the way most of the walkers went, which was up to the corner where Ms. Post was, orange-vested, waving cars by, blowing her whistle until her face looked like it would pop, Cynthia walked through the grass and headed around the back of the school to take the shortcut. She could've gone through the back door, which would've been an even shorter cut, but then she would've missed snapping on Greg, and who could avoid the opportunity to roast? Plus, she'd learned from her grandfather a long time ago how important tradition was.

She walked along the side of the school, dragging her fingers on the red brick of the building until she reached the line of trees at the back. Not exactly a forest, just a single line of maples that created a barrier between the school and the road. When Cynthia reached the tree line, the trees thick with limbs that looked less like arms and more like outstretched legs—thick-rooted yoga trees—she hiked her jeans up above her ankles and tip-toed, because the land seemed to always be muddy there.

On the other side of the trees was Carigan Street, known for nothing besides the entrance to the Southview Cemetery. The cemetery had a regal iron gate wrapped around it and took up the entire block. Cynthia, after looking both ways, ran across the street and into the cemetery because through the graveyard was the shortest way home. No point in going around when she could go through. Plus, she had to get giggles for her grandfather.

Giggles were cigarette butts. Cinder collected them and Cynthia always tried to make sure to find some if she could. People were always walking through the cemetery, smoking and leaving their leftover cigs on the ground and sometimes even leaving them on the gravestones along with flowers, pictures, notes, bottles, and candles. But the giggles were what she was looking for. What Cinder always wanted. But he hadn't named them that. Cynthia had.

Shortly after Miss Fran died, Cynthia was helping her grandfather clean the apartment. Helping him orga-nize his papers and clothes. Helping him straighten up.

"You want this?" she asked, holding up an old Vietnam veteran's hat.

"Uh-huh."

"These?" Cynthia asked, holding up a stack of stamps and envelopes.

"Hmmm. I ain't mailing nothing, so . . . nah," Cinder said. Cynthia peeled one of the stamps from the book, stuck it on her forehead, then made a funny face at her grandfather. He smiled and she put the rest of the stamps in her back pocket.

"What about all this?" she then said, holding up an ashtray full of cigarette butts, red lipstick smudged on the tips.

He looked, leaned into the ashtray, kinda looked like he was leaning over the ledge of a pool, threatening to fall in. He picked one up, looked at it like he was looking at a single bullet. One that could explode his heart. But didn't. At least not in the way Cynthia thought. Cinder's eyes watered, but he didn't cry. He giggled.

Cynthia traipsed around the cemetery, looking for giggles, finding none. There were people walking their dogs through the graveyard, others visiting their family members, sweeping their areas, picking up trash, replacing dead flowers with live ones. Cynthia saw two girls sitting on a skateboard in front of a tombstone. She thought she recognized them but didn't want to stare because it would've been weird. She kept walking.

Kept looking, eyes running across the tops of the stones that had last names engraved in them.

But she was running out of time.

It was 3:26 p.m. Seven minutes until the Say-So show, so she figured she may have struck out this time. She may not have any new giggles to give her grandfather. But then she came to Miss Fran's grave. And sitting on top of it was a cigarette butt. Lipstick kissed the end of it. Cynthia took it as a sign, slid it into her pocket, and headed on.

After she came out on the other end of the cemetery—the Southview Avenue side—she crossed the street over to where the playground was. There was a little girl sitting on a swing, kicking her legs, flying back and forth, static electricity for hair, happiness for a face.

But she was the only person there.

And it was 3:31 p.m.

Cynthia sat on Cinder's Block. Stretched to crack her back. The couch seemed to be making her body old. And when she thought about that, it made her laugh.

"I bet the reason a couch is called a couch is because of the ouch part," she said to herself. Or maybe to the swinging girl, but the swinging girl was swinging and not listening. "Yeah . . . that's not a good one."

3:32 p.m.

A bird landed next to her. A pigeon. A dingy gray that was still somehow beautiful, like clouds before rain.

"Yeah, I always wing it anyway," she said to the bird. "I wonder what it must be like to be you. It's like, you got wings. So you can fly anywhere you want to go, which is pretty much the most amazing thing ever. You can fly to the things you want. But the letdown is that when you get to wherever the things you want are, you ain't got the hands to grab it." That one made her laugh a little.

3:33 p.m.

No one came. But no one *ever* came. Well, that's not true. Sometimes Gregory Pitts, Remy Vaughn, Joey Santiago, and Candace Greene would come, but that's just because they lived in Southview too. Cynthia figured her low attendance was because people had to go home after school. You know, parents, practice, homework . . . stuff like that. Either that, or they never thought she was being serious about her shows. That the whole 3:33 thing was just part of her act. Part of the joke. Part of the Say-So thing, and so they all were thinking, "Yeah okay, if you say so." Right? Of course.

Truth was, 3:33 p.m. was for Cynthia's mother. She got off work as a barista at three and had school— now graduate school—at four fifteen. She always went straight to class, but if for some reason she decided to skip, to take a day off, to give herself a break, Cynthia would be right there, standing on Cinder's Block ready to joke a smile onto her hero's face, just the way her *super*hero had taught her.

But there are no days off for a hero.

So Cynthia opened her backpack, pulled her notebook out and snatched a page loose. She dug out a pen and started scribbling the joke about the bird and it not having hands and how awesome it would be to have wings if you also had hands, but then that would make birds angels and how it would be way too scary to see angels with beaks. That made her laugh too.

Cynthia then pulled out an envelope. And a stamp. She kept them in the small pocket in the front of her bag. She folded the paper, slid it into the envelope, sealed it, then wrote her own address on it. After that, she slapped the stamp on it. She peeled another stamp from the book and walked over to the little girl on the swing.

"Want a sticker?" Cynthia asked.

The little girl stopped swinging. Held her hand out. Cynthia stuck the sticky square to the back of it. Charlie Chaplin.

When she got upstairs to her apartment, Cynthia dropped her bag on the couch and beelined to her grandfather's room.

Knocked.

"Grandpa, I got mail."

No answer.

Knocked again.

"Grandpa. It's Say-So. Mail."

Nothing.

Concerned, Cynthia turned the knob, opened the door slowly. "Grandpa?"

He was there, sitting on the side of his bed, scribbling in his notepad. Paper balls littered the floor, so many that the door swept a bunch of them to the side of the room. That wasn't unusual. There were always paper balls. Most with random sentences on them. Starts and stops. His hands holding a pen, spitting whatever was coming from his sputtering mind. But a few were not in his handwriting. A few had been snatched from envelopes written in the loopy cursive of the coolest granddaughter in world.

"Grandpa, you hear me knocking?" Cynthia asked. Cinder looked up at her, and for a moment it seemed like he didn't recognize her.

Finally, "Oh, Say-So. I didn't hear you. In here trying to get my jokes together. Trying to write a zinger for you to take to school tomorrow, y'know?" Cynthia came to his side. Kissed his cheek, looked down at the paper. All he had written was the word "EARDRUMS."

"Eardrums, huh?"

"Yeah, it's not working." He ripped it out, balled it up, tossed it on the floor. "I got something else I think is better, but I don't know. Anyway, how was school?"

"I killed."

"You did the shirt joke?"

"Yep. And it crushed 'em."

"Ah. Your mother used to love that joke." His voice sweetened for a moment. Then he continued. "Your teacher ain't get mad, did she?"

"No, no, she was cool about it," Cynthia reassured him, remembering the cigarette butt in her pocket. "Oh, I almost forgot. I found a giggle." She pulled the red-stained tip from her pocket, dropped it in his palm. Cinder let it roll around, staring down at it for a second before smiling. He got up from the bed and dropped it in a bottle on a small table a few feet away, adding it to what looked like a hundred. Maybe more. "And some mail came for you."

Cynthia held the envelope out. The one that she'd stuffed with the paper she'd written the bird joke on. The one that she'd simply written her own address—which was his address—on. Nothing else. Grandpa took the envelope and set it on the table. Cynthia knew that later he would open it, read it, then forget he'd read it, and believe he wrote it. And the next day he'd tell her to try a new joke in Mrs. Stevens's class. And she'd tell him she would, then come home and tell him his jokes were working. His jokes were still cracking people up. And he'd say things like, "We a good team, ain't we?" Or, "Like father, like daughter." And Cynthia would kiss his cheek and nod.

Cynthia headed back toward his bedroom door.

Before leaving she turned and asked, "What was the other thing?" Cinder looked confused, so Cynthia continued. "The joke. You said you were thinking about something else."

"Oh, just this thing I was kicking around. But I don't think it'll work."

"What was it? Tell me."

"Okay." Cinder steadied himself. Looked his granddaughter in the eye. "What would happen if a school bus fell from the sky?"

Cynthia thought for a second, a smile creeping onto her lips. "I mean . . . is it coming from Ookabooka Land?"

Silence.

Just that thought between them. Cynthia looking at her grandfather, her Cinderella, her cinder block. The man who taught her to perform. Taught her that life is funny most of the time, and the times it ain't funny are even funnier. And there ain't no forgetting that.

He looked back at her. And in a way that only grandfather and granddaughter could do, together Cynthia and Cinder split open and laughter poured out of them. A laughter free enough to make the bottle (of giggles) on the table rattle.

HOW A BOY
CAN BECOME A
GREASE FIRE

GREGORY PITTS'S friends love him so much that they
told him the truth. And the truth was, he smelled
dead. Like, rotten. It wasn't that he *was* rotten, but just
that he smelled like his body had mistaken its organs
for garbage and that he was essentially a walking,
talking trash can. And on this, of all days, that smell
just wasn't going to cut it. So in an act of service and
sheer desperation, Remar Vaughn, Joey Santiago, and
Candace Greene—Gregory's crew—decide to help him
out. Because today was a day of romance.

"Before we get going, you sure you good, Candace?"
Joey asked. "I heard what happened to Bryson." Bryson
was Candace's cousin. He'd gotten jumped the day
before.

"Yeah, it's cool. Bry's a tough kid," Candace said. "Plus, we walking that way, so as soon as we get done with lover boy here, I'm gonna stop by and see him."

"Cool, well . . . first thing we need to do is get you smellin' right," Remar, who they all called Remy, said to Gregory. They had all met up by the benches in the front of the school.

"You got the stuff, right?" Candace asked Remy.

"You know it."

"What is it? And why y'all talking about it like it's . . ." Gregory caught himself. "Know what? It don't even matter as long as it works."

"Oh, it'll work," Joey said, bouncing his eyebrows.

Remy dug around his backpack and pulled out a can of body spray. "Now, Justin gets this stuff from the gas station. He says it's basically deodorant for your whole body." Justin was Remy's older brother, and he was always right, let Remy tell it. He popped the top off the canister. "Close your eyes."

And then . . . *pssssszzzzzzzzzz*. He sprayed Gregory from the top of his head to the bottom of his feet. A spritz or two even got in his mouth, sending Gregory gagging and coughing.

"Hold still!" Candace ordered, while Remy spun Gregory around and sprayed all down his back. It smelled like . . . it smelled like . . . a combination of burnt flowers and burnt rubber. But that was better than Gregory's normal smell, the smell of all-day *fownk*.

"No spraying!" Ms. Wockley yelled, pointing at Gregory and his friends. "You know the rules. Go away if you want to spray!" Ms. Wockley's frustration came from the fact that there was always someone spraying something in the hallway. Always a perfume or cologne that was supposed to help but ended up taking stink up to stank. But this was a special case. Either way, Ms. Wockley's outrage was hilarious to Gregory, Remy, Joey, and Candace, so the four of them cracked all the way up.

"Go away if you want to spray!" Candace repeated with a hoot. "She a poet and she don't know it!"

"A rapper that look like a napper!" Remy followed.

"A spitter way too bitter!" Joey came in third.

All their jokes matched the corniness of Ms. Wockley's non-joke, which made them laugh even harder, Gregory half choking because laugh plus spray equals choke.

They started walking, but they weren't walking home like they normally did. They lived in the Southview Apartments, but decided today that they would walk over to Rogers Street because that's where Sandra White lived. Gregory had been trying to work up the courage to tell her that he liked her and wanted to know if maybe they could be boyfriend and girlfriend even though he hated the way that sounded. Sounded . . . trash. *Together* was what he preferred to call it. He had told Remy, Joey, and Candace that he wanted to do this, and they were in full support and along for the ride. Not to mention, Candace was the only one who knew where Sandra lived. She and Sandra were closer when they were younger, but they were still cool.

Even though they were all in support of Gregory shooting his shot, they also told him that he'd need to prepare. He'd need to make sure he was ready, and to put his best foot forward, first and foremost, he needed to not smell like a . . . forward foot. He needed to smell better than the lunchroom. Better than the locker room.

"Yeah, so I just hit you with the *ooh*, and now you ready for some *la la*," Remy said. He was always saying corny stuff like that, mainly because he swore he was some kind of mastermind when it came to approaching girls—thanks to Justin—even though Candace told him every chance she got that he wasn't.

"I think you hit him with too much *ooh*. Like . . . smells more like *eww*," Candace joked, curling her top lip up under her nostrils. But it was better than before. And since the smell part was worked out, it was time for her to explain the importance of moisturizing.

"Now that you don't stink, we gotta make sure you ain't dry." Candace pulled a bottle of lotion the size of a shoe out of her backpack. Gregory's eyes widened, and his brows furrowed, leaving him with a look of astonishment. And . . . fear.

"What the . . . ? Where you get that?" he yawped, slowly relaxing his forehead.

"Found this in my mother's bathroom," Candace explained as they walked up to the corner, where Ms. Post, the crossing guard, stood. Ms. Post blew the whistle, and they all walked across the street and to the left, heading down Portal Avenue.

"Hold up so I can do this," Candace said. "Can't walk and lotion at the same time." The boys held up while Candace pumped the lotion into her hand, jamming the plunger down over and over again until she had enough to turn sidewalk to Slip 'N Slide. "Let's start with them paws," she said, reaching out for Gregory's right hand. She began with his fingertips, then worked her way up, making sure to give extra attention to the webbing in between, which made Gregory snicker. Then on to his wrist, up his forearm, and then she stopped. "Elbows are important."

"Elbows?" Gregory was confused.

"Elbows," Joey chimed in.

"You don't want Sandra thinking your elbows so dry that your arm is going to crack and break in half if you try to hug her, do you?" Candace asked, all kinds of serious.

"I mean, that wouldn't happen." Gregory looked at Joey and Remy. They didn't say a word, so he repeated himself. "That . . . wouldn't happen, right?"

Joey just dropped his chin. "Wow."

"What?" Now Gregory was really confused.

"'That wouldn't happen,' he says," Remy scoffed. "Did everybody hear that? He said, that wouldn't happen! Let me tell you something, Gregory Pitts. I've heard stories, horror stories, about dry boys who try to be romantic and they end up a pile of paint chips. You don't want to be paint chips, my brother, do you?"

"No."

"Then let me do my magic on these elbows," Candace commanded. Then she went to work, first on his right elbow. Circles with center of her palm, then pincher-claw rubs with the tips of her fingers for optimal moisturizing. When his arm was as shiny as Mr. Davanzo's bald head, she started over, this time with the left hand, fingers, wrist, forearm, and again . . . elbow.

"Okay," Gregory said, pulling away, a little embarrassed by the attention, plus, people were walking by watching Gregory get worked on like some kind of car. But he could feel the difference. His fingers felt like they'd been freed from casts. Lotion. Who knew?

"Not done yet." Candace pumped more lotion from the bottle.

"Not done?" he squawked. "What good is all this if we don't ever make it to her house?"

"We will," Joey assured him.

"And the real question is, what good is it making it

to her house when all she going to do is wonder why your hands and elbows glistening and your face looks like you just got jumped by seventeen giant pieces of chalk and they only gave you head shots?" Remy threw fake punches in the air.

"Exactly," Candace said, another glob of lotion piled in her hand. "Come here." Gregory came a little closer as Candace rubbed her hands together. Then she slapped them on his cheeks. Gregory squirmed, but Candace wouldn't let up, pressing at his face like she was trying to rub smudges off of fresh sneakers, getting the creases of his nose and the corners of his mouth. Oh, and his earlobes. Even Remy and Joey were a little puzzled by that one, but they figured Candace knew what she was doing.

A school bus pulled up to the stop sign at that corner. The clack of a window dropping.

"Hey!" a boy from the bus yelled. Candace, Remy, and Joey turned and looked, but not Gregory. Candace clasped his face in her hands. "You might as well give up. No matter how hard you try, that ug-mug won't come off!" The boy spoke like his tongue was too big for his mouth, spit flying everywhere.

"Thank God," Candace shouted. "Because it might look like *yours* underneath!"

"Then we'd really be in trouble!" Remy followed. Joey didn't say nothing. Just started searching the ground for a rock or something to throw, but the bus moved on.

Candace brushed it off, then went back to business, rubbing her palm on Gregory's forehead, polishing it. "There," she said at last, stepping back, admiring her work. "You look . . . not bad." That was as far as she could go. Any compliment more than that was gross.

"I'm ready?" Gregory asked, eyeing Candace's backpack nervously.

"Almost," Joey said, now unzipping *his* backpack.

"What now?" Gregory took two steps backward.

"Well, here's the thing. There's only really one other thing you need to be ready for this. Something for your lips."

"What?!" Gregory took two more steps backward.

"Relax. I'm just saying chapped lips—"

"Are gross," Candace finished. "Like . . . for real."

"I mean, seriously, what if we get to her house, you lay it all out on the table about how you feel about her and how you would like to get her phone number and blah, blah, blah, and she says, who cares about a phone number. Give me a kiss." Joey bounced his eyebrows.

"Hold on. Just so we clear, she won't say that," Candace clarified.

"How you know?" Remy chimed.

"Trust me. She won't. But she might be like oh, he takes care of himself. Maybe one day I'll give him a kiss."

"Your first smooch," Remy teased like he'd kissed anybody, but he hadn't.

"But if your lips look like they look right now, which is white with that weird burn ring around your mouth—" Joey started, but Candace cut him off.

"Stop licking your lips so much, bro. It's gross and it makes you smell like spit, which when added to the underarm stench makes you smell like throw up, and as your friend and as a girl who happens to unfortunately like boys, I'm telling you it's a deal breaker." Candace's words sizzled, stung.

"Wow . . . thanks for your honesty . . . I guess," Gregory said.

"It's 'cause I love you," Candace said, shrugging.

"So, with that being said . . ." Joey pulled his hand out of his bag. In it was a ziplock bag of goop. "Got this from my mom's room. It don't come like this. I just couldn't risk taking the whole container out of there, because she would know, and ultimately, murder me. And I don't wanna die before Gregory gets a kiss."

"Or before you get one," Remy said.

"Or before *you* get one," Joey shot back.

"Wait. Hold up." Gregory got back to business. "I gotta use all that?!"

"No!" From Candace.

"Noooo!" From Remy.

"Come on, man," Joey said with a laugh, pulling the bag open, the scent of menthol wafting out. "Now, this is medicated stuff, so take it easy."

"Why? If it's medicated, then it should be good for me," Gregory said, dipping his fingers in. And before Joey could reply, Gregory slapped the glob on his mouth and started rubbing it in.

Joey's mouth dropped open.

"What?" Gregory asked, and a nanosecond later said, "Oh." And then, "Oh . . . wait. Oh. *Ohhh.*" He started fanning his mouth with his hand. "It . . . burns," he said, his eyes starting to water.

"What you mean, it burns?" Candace asked, hands on hips.

"Joey, what you give him?" Remy snatched the bag, scooped out a fingertip of the slime. Sniffed. "Is this . . . ?" Sniffed again. Held out his finger for Candace to smell. "Is this—"

"VapoRub?" Candace snatched the bag and took a big huff. It opened her chest immediately. Joey nodded sheepishly.

"Why would you give him VapoRub?" Remy pretended to slap Joey on the head.

"We ain't have Vaseline, but this stuff got Vaseline *in* it, so I figured it's basically the same," Joey explained.

"Dude, that's the stuff my mother rubs on me when I'm sick, and it goes into my skin and makes the whole inside of my body cold," Remy said.

"And don't your chest be greasy after she do it?" Joey asked.

"I mean . . ."

"Exactly." Joey gave one single hard nod.

"Not the same, Joey." Candace's face was somewhere between amused and annoyed.

"How was I supposed to know he was gonna treat it like pudding!"

"Burning, guys. Burning, burning, burning," Gregory panted. Candace and Remy began fanning Gregory's mouth too.

"Just imagine it's the burning sensation in your heart for Sandra." Joey pinched the bag closed inch by inch.

Remy leaned in to Gregory's ear, almost whispering in a fake hypnotic voice, "Sannnnnndra." Then, because he couldn't help it, he added, "Sorry, man."

And with that, they continued on, down Portal Avenue, until they got to Rogers Street, the whole way gassing Gregory up, trying to take his mind off his fire lips by telling him how much they believed in him and how Sandra will too.

"What's not to love?" Candace said, doing everything she could to keep a straight face. And when they finally got to Sandra's house, Remy, Joey, and Candace hung back.

"You ready?" Remy asked Gregory.

"I . . . think so," Gregory said, his lips still tingling. He pulled a piece of paper from his pocket, walked up the steps to Sandra's house, rang the doorbell, then ran back down the steps because Candace had been telling him how girls don't like when you're all in their space.

"You don't gotta be this far away, fool," she muttered, nudging him forward.

The door opened. Sandra poked her head out, looking confused. She still had on the sweat shirt she'd worn to school. Light blue. Yellow rectangles. A pattern that through Gregory's watery eyes (from his burning lips!) looked like a bunch of school buses falling from the sky.

"Wassup y'all?" she said, cocking her head, clearly trying to figure out what was going on. Gregory said nothing. Just stood there, shiny, shaking.

"Greg," Remy prompted, put his hand on Gregory's back. Another nudge.

"Greg got something to tell you, Sandra. Right, Greg?" This was from Candace.

Gregory nodded. Unfolded the paper. Started reading.

"Sandra, you always get questions right in class, and I think that's . . . good. And you never say nothing bad about me, at least not to my face, and so, I just wanted to know if I could have your phone number."

Candace looked at Joey. Joey at Remy. Remy at Joey at Candace at Gregory. They couldn't believe he'd done it. They couldn't believe he'd just asked her.

Sandra walked down the steps, came right up on Gregory. Twitched her nose, squinted as if the light bouncing off Gregory's shiny forehead was blinding her. He kept pursing his lips and blowing.

"What you doing?" Sandra asked. "You ain't . . . trying to blow no kisses, are you?"

"No, no!" Gregory's voice jumped an octave. Maybe two. Almost whistle-high. "I wouldn't . . . It's just . . . um . . . my lips are burning."

"Oh . . . uh . . . why?"

"VapoRub."

"Why you put that on your lips?"

"I don't . . . It's hard to explain."

"Why you so greasy?"

"That's hard to explain too."

"Why you smell like that?"

"That's—"

"Hard to explain?" Sandra finished for him. Gregory nodded. "Can you try?"

Gregory's hands started shaking, the paper vibrating like dry leaves in the wind. He looked down and started reading his note of compliments again.

Halfway through, he glanced up. Sandra was smiling. And Gregory thought maybe it was the kind of smile that came just before laughing.

Then Gregory thought, *But maybe not.*

THE CORNER OF **PORTAL AVE.**

THE
BROOM
DOG

A SCHOOL bus is many things.

A school bus is a substitute for a limousine. More class. A school bus is a classroom with a substitute teacher. A school bus is the students' version of a teachers' lounge. A school bus is the principal's desk. A school bus is the nurse's cot. A school bus is an office with all the phones ringing. A school bus is a command center. A school bus is a pillow fort that rolls. A school bus is a tank reshaped— hot dogs and baloney are the same meat. A school bus is a science lab—hot dogs and baloney are the same meat. A school bus is a safe zone. A school bus is a war zone. A school bus is a concert hall. A school bus is a food court. A school bus is a court of law, all judges, all jury. A school bus is a magic show full of disappearing acts. Saw someone in half. Pick a card, any card. Pass it to the person next to you. *He like you. She like you. K-i-s-s-i . . . s-s-i-p-p-i* is only funny on a school bus. A school bus is a stage. A school bus is a stage play. A school bus is a spelling bee. A speaking bee. A *get your hand out my face* bee. A *your breath smell like sour turnips* bee. A *you don't even know what a turnip is* bee. A *maybe not, but I know what a turn up is and your breath smell all the way turnt up* bee. A school bus is a bumblebee, buzzing around with a bunch of stingers on the inside of it. Windows for wings that flutter up and down like the windows inside Chinese restaurants and post offices in neighborhoods where school buses are spaceships. A school bus is a book of stamps. Passing mail through windows. Notes in the form of candy wrappers telling the street something sweet came by. Notes in the form of sneaky middle fingers. Notes in the form of fingers pointing at the world zooming by. A school bus is a paintbrush painting the world a blurry brushstroke. A school bus is also wet paint. Good for adding an extra coat, but it will dirty you if you lean against it, if you get too comfortable. A school bus is a reclining chair. In the kitchen. Nothing cool about it but makes perfect sense. A school bus is a dirty fridge. A school bus is cheese. A school bus is a ketchup packet with a tiny hole in it. Left on a seat. A plastic fork-knife-spoon. A paper tube around a straw. That straw will puncture the lid on things, make the world drink something with some fizz and fight. Something delightful and uncomfortable. Something that will stain. And cause gas. A school bus is a fast food joint with extra value and no food. Order taken. Take a number. Send a text to the person sitting next you. There is so much trouble to get into. *Have you ever thought about opening the back door? My mother not home till five thirty. I can't. I got dance practice at four.* A school bus is a talent show. *I got dance practice right now. On this bus.* A school bus is a microphone. A beat machine. A recording booth. A school bus is a horn section. A rhythm section. An orchestra pit. A balcony to shoot paper ball three-pointers from. A school bus is a basketball court. A football stadium. A soccer field. Sometimes a boxing ring. A school bus is a movie set. Actors, directors, producers, script. Scenes. Settings. Motivations. Action! Cut. *Your fake tears look real. These are real tears. But I thought we were making a comedy.* A school bus is a misunderstanding. A school bus is a masterpiece that everyone pretends to understand. A school bus is the mountain range behind Mona Lisa. The Sphinx's nose. An unknown wonder of the world. An unknown wonder to Canton Post, who heard bus riders talk about their journeys to and from school. But to Canton, a school bus is also a cannonball. A thing that almost destroyed him. Almost made him motherless.

His mother is the crossing guard at Latimer Middle School and has been the crossing guard there since before he was born. He grew up running around their house wearing her neon vest, blowing her whistle. He learned to say "stop" before he learned to say "potty." Hand up to halt. Then hand out for the wave-through. To Canton, crossing guards, especially his mother, seemed to have special powers. They were able to stop moving things. Able to slow traffic. Able to make a safe way for people to cross from one side to another. Their vests were like capes, and their whistles blew some kind of magic tone that forced drivers to hit brakes.

That's what Canton always thought. Until a year ago when a little blue ball went bouncing off the sidewalk into the street. And a boy, the size of a big baby, named Kenzi Thompson, went running after it. Canton's mom had turned her back just for a moment, a split second, and by the time she realized what was happening, Kenzi was charging across the crosswalk, a school bus heading right toward him. There wasn't enough time to blow the whistle, so Canton's mother, Ms. Post, went chasing after Kenzi, who, once he realized a bus was coming, froze in the middle of Portal Avenue. The bus hit the brakes. The scream of metal and smoke kicking up from the burning rubber filled the air as Ms. Post threw her entire body into Kenzi, knocking him forward, the bus turning just enough to avoid hitting

Kenzi but not enough to avoid slightly bumping her.

But a slight bump from a bus ain't so slight.

But a broken shoulder and a bruised hip is much better than a burial.

But the whole thing was completely devastating to Canton.

Canton always waited for his mother after school, killing time by helping Mr. Munch, the custodian, do custodial things. Actually, mostly Canton just sat around the front of the building listening to Mr. Munch complain about things like the school bathrooms.

"Why can't y'all hit the toilet, Canton? I mean, the hole is huge and somehow y'all figure out how to get pee all over the seat. All over the floor. All over the walls. *How?*"

But on the day Canton's mother was hit by a bus, the conversation about why kids throw pennies on the floor like pennies don't spend was cut short by Jasmine Jordan and Terrence Jumper, who came running back into the school screaming about it.

"Ms. Post got hit by a school bus!" A sentence Canton never expected to hear. Never wanted to hear. And hearing it was like hearing the world's longest whistle blow, shrill, shredding his eardrums. His skin was crawling, felt like it was changing color, from brown to yellow. School bus yellow. By the time Canton and Mr. Munch got outside, sirens were already blaring down Portal.

Ms. Post was back to work in a week. Whistle in mouth, vest strapped on, altered only by the sling holding her shoulder in place. She went back to normal. She had to. Said it was just part of the job.

But not Canton. He didn't go back to normal.

The afternoon his mother returned to the corner to guide students across the street, Mr. Munch found Canton in the bathroom after school, sitting on the nasty tile floor in the corner. His head pressed against his knees.

"Canton, what you doing in here?" Mr. Munch asked, realizing he wasn't actually . . . using the bathroom. And when Canton lifted his head up, Mr. Munch could see that he'd been crying. He could also see that Canton's chest was pumping, heaving like it was hard for him to breathe. Like it would break open. Mr. Munch got down on the floor with him. Squatted beside him and talked him through some breathing exercises.

"Come on, Canton. Count to ten with me. One, two, three . . ." And then, "Now let's go back to one. Ten, nine, eight . . ." And eventually Canton could breathe. Could talk. Could stand. Mr. Munch walked him outside. When they made it to the corner, where Ms. Post was working, Canton wrapped his arms around his mother and squeezed. Held her so tight that she winced, her shoulder still a sack of broken bone.

"Okay. I'm okay. You're okay. We're okay," she

chanted in his ear, trying to figure out how to get him to let go so she could do her job, but also not wanting to let him go because he was also her job.

Mr. Munch patted Canton on his shoulder, but realizing there was no way this boy would let go of his mother, Mr. Munch decided he would take over for her, step into the street, stick his fingers in his mouth and whistle even louder than the whistle around Ms. Post's neck.

He put his hand up and yelled at the cars, "I'm tellin' y'all right now, you hit me and I'm hitting you back!" And once the traffic stopped, he yelled for all the waiting students to "get on 'cross the street." Then he turned back toward the stopped cars and puffed his chest, almost bucking, daring them to move.

The next day, Mr. Munch met Canton outside of his last class of the day, Mr. Davanzo's social studies class. In his hand was a big push broom.

"How you feeling?"

"I'm okay."

"Still got the jitters?"

Canton nodded, just slightly, trying to hide his embarrassment.

"Wanna take a walk with me? I wanna give you something."

Canton and Mr. Munch sauntered the halls of the school, pushing dust, and hair that looked like dust, and coins and candy wrappers and a random sock and drawstrings and loose braids and who knows what else, as all the other students bustled around, eventually funneling through the double doors into the outside world.

Pushing. Brooming. Mr. Munch, talking.

"When my daughter, Winnie, went off to college, my wife got so nervous that she'd call Winnie every single day, multiple times a day. And whenever Winnie wouldn't answer, Zena would just . . . lose it," Mr. Munch started.

"Zena's your wife?"

"Yeah." Mr. Munch grinned. "Best person I ever known. Kinda gotta be to deal with a man that comes home every day smelling like bleach and urine. But she's been through a lot. Seen a lot of the world when she was young, and it made her terrified for our daughter. Made her anxious about every step Winnie took away from us. What if something happens to her? What if she needs us? What if she's in danger? Zena would go on and on with these kinds of questions, up all night, sick with fear all day."

"And what you say?"

"Nothing. But what I *did* was buy her a dog."

"A dog?"

"Yep." Canton and Mr. Munch stopped at the custodian closet. The old man pushed the pile of middle school debris into the corner, then pulled out a million keys, flipping through them like pages of a book. "Not because she needed something else to care for—no dog can take the place of our baby girl—but I read this thing about emotional support animals."

"What's that?"

"Well, okay, first, I should clarify that my daughter called me and told me about them without my wife knowing, and *then* I read about them myself. Basically, it's like having a dog to make you feel better." Finally, he picked the right key and opened the closet door. "I mean, what's better than a dog, right?"

They went into the custodian's closet, which was big enough to be an office. Pictures on the wall of Mr. Munch's wife and daughter. And the dog. A small curly-haired thing with an underbite so ugly it was cute. At least Canton thought so. But besides its cuteness, Canton kept thinking about all the things *better* than dogs. To him. Like ice cream. And skateboards. And maybe a girlfriend one day. Or even a girl that's a friend. And a good joke. Oh, and video games. Then, after all that . . . dogs were cool.

"Mr. Munch, why you telling me all this?" Canton asked, done running down the better-than list in his mind. He was thinking maybe Mr. Munch was trying to be *his* emotional support dog, except not a dog. His emotional support human, and that all this was just a way to keep his mind off his mother and the fear of a school bus swiping her again.

"Why am I telling you this?" He repeated Canton's question. Then he opened a locker that stood in the corner of the closet/office. "Because I made you one."

"You . . . you made me a *dog*?"

"Well . . . I mean . . . real emotional support dogs aren't allowed in school, unfortunately. Plus, I couldn't just buy you a dog. Your mom might not be okay with that. But I thought maybe this could help." Mr. Munch reached into the locker and pulled out the head of a broom—the sweeping part—which he'd detached from the broomstick. The straw was curled and mangled as if Mr. Munch had been cleaning the sidewalk for, like, twenty years with it. He had drawn big black circles on one side like eyes. And an oval with a tic-tac-toe board in the middle of it, which Canton assumed was supposed to be the mouth. At the top, two small pieces of dustcloth, cut into ears and glued in place.

"It's . . . a . . . broom."

"But I cleaned it. Promise. And yeah, it's a broom, until you do this." He petted the wiry twine as if it were fur. As if he were scratching behind the ear of a Yorkie in desperate need of grooming. The straw popped back up when he was done, just like a dog's would.

"Why is the mouth like that? Is the . . . broom . . . dog angry?"

"No." Mr. Munch turned the broom head toward him, shrugged. "He's smiling."

"Oh." Canton squished up his befuddled face, decided to take Mr. Munch's word about the smile, but was still unsure about everything else. "So, you really think this gonna help me?"

"Can't hurt to try?" A slick smirk crept onto Mr. Munch's face. "I mean, the worst that could happen is you decide to clean up the street. So either way . . . everybody wins."

The next day, after school, Canton, with the broom dog tucked under his arm, slowly walked up to the corner to watch his mother—to guard the crossing guard. He leaned against the stop sign at the corner. And whenever Ms. Post had to step into the street, blow her whistle, raise her hand to stop traffic, whenever Canton's chest would become an inflated balloon, he would run his fingers through the broom dog's hair.

Eventually, he named it Dusty.

It's strange, the things that work.

It's been a year since Mr. Munch gave Canton the broom dog. A year since the first panic attack. A year and a week since the accident, and things have gotten better.

The bell rings, and everyone gets up to leave Mr. Davanzo's class.

The big guy, Simeon, stands at the door, giving everyone high fives like he always does.

"Up high," he says to Canton as he approaches. Canton slaps his hand.

"Don't forget tonight's homework. We're talking geography. Write about place. Write about people. Human environmental interaction!" Mr. Davanzo shouted over the end-of-day clamor.

Canton stops at his locker. Reaches in to grab Dusty, then heads for the door. He passes Ms. Wockley in the hallway scolding Simeon (the giant he'd just given a five), and Kenzi Thompson, the blue ball in his hand. Outside he walks past a kid he'd never seen before sitting on the bench by the door, wearing some kind of green suit. At the bench next to him was Candace Greene—his crush—who he never had the courage to talk to because she was always with her friends, Dumb Joey, Stinky Greg, and Cool Remy. And next to them on the third bench was this kid Britton Burns and his crew the Low Cuts, who were known around school for pocket pat-downs for pennies.

"Wassup, Canton?" Trista, one of the Low Cuts and the toughest girl anyone had ever known, said. Canton waved, kept walking, passed Mr. Johnson moving the carpool line along. Had to get to the corner before the first cross. That was his thing. For a year and a week. And when Canton finally made it up to the crosswalk at Portal Avenue, there was his mother, Ms. Post, strapping on her vest and pulling the whistle attached to a black lanyard over her head like it was some kind of prestigious medal.

"There's my sweet boy," she said, greeting him, arm winged. They hugged. "How was school?"

"It was okay."

"Homework?"

"A little. Ms. Broome wants us to imagine ourselves as a thing. And Mr. Davanzo wants us to record human environmental interaction."

"Which is . . . ?"

"Which is what I'm gonna work on." Canton made a funny face at his mom, and she made one back.

"I'm not exactly sure what that means, but I feel like I'm probably an expert at it."

Canton chuckled. "I'll let you know if I need your assistance."

"Deal. Well, get to it." Ms. Post winked. Canton pulled a notebook from his backpack, along with Dusty the broom dog, then set the bag down against the stop sign so he could sit and have a little cushion. The broom dog rested on his lap as he scribbled words and phrases trying to describe the environment around him.

Latimer Middle School.

Corner.

Portal Avenue.

Cars.

Classmates.

Mom.

Whistle.

People stop.

People go.

People talk.

People hug.

People frown.

People laugh.

People go off.

People go on.

Canton glanced up as everyone gradually congregated at the corner, like water building against a dam, allowed to flow every few minutes. People turning and crossing, waiting and talking. The web of conversations. Gregory Pitts liked Sandra White. Satchmo Jenkins feared he might be eaten by a dog on his way home. Cynthia Sower was putting on a show at 3:33 p.m. Some banter on boogers, and everyone wanted to know what secret things Fatima Moss was always writing.

He watched his classmates tap-dance with tongues, challenging one another, slipping and sliding from story to story. Watched his mother perform a kind of ballet. How she spun, stepped into the street like she was made of more. Blew her whistle. Put a hand up for a bus to stop. Put a hand out to wave the walkers through.

When everyone had gone, when all the Latimer students had walked off, headed home or wherever they went after school, Ms. Post stood at the corner, removed her vest. She slung it over her shoulder. Pulled the whistle over her head. Another day, job done.

"Ready to walk?" she asked Canton, who had been working nonstop on his assignment.

He nodded. "Yeah."

Canton stood, the broom dog falling from his lap like he had forgotten it was there. Ms. Post picked it up.

"Sheesh. This thing has seen better days." She examined it. The mangled straw. The pieces of felt that were meant to be ears long gone. "You know, I know it's supposed to be a dog, but if you look at it now, it kinda looks like a bus." She handed it to Canton, then pointed out the similarities. "The eyes are like the headlights, and the mean mouth—"

"It's a smile," Canton corrected her.

"Oh, right. The smile . . . is like the grille. Funny."

Canton had never noticed that. The broom dog had just become a thing he had, a thing he knew was there if he needed it, but it had been a long time, he just now realized, since he'd actually needed it.

"It's all faded now anyway," Canton said, grabbing

his backpack. They stood on the corner, looked both ways before crossing.

"Still want it?" his mother asked. Canton shrugged, tossed it up in the air. Caught it. Tossed it again. Caught it. Again, and loose straw separated from the bunch. Again. And more loose straw, falling down on them. And more. Ms. Post laughed. "Look at that. A school bus falling from the sky."

Canton smiled, knowing a school bus is many things. So is a walk home.

"A FOOT LEAVES, A FOOT LANDS,
AND OUR LONGING GIVES IT
MOMENTUM FROM REST TO REST."

—GARNETTE CADOGAN

ACKNOWLEDGMENTS

There are always people to thank because there are always people helping to make books come true, like dreams. People who help make the book a thing, and people who help make the stories.

In the bookmaker category, I, of course, have to thank my editor, Caitlyn, who trusts me as much as I trust her. Means the world to me. My agent, Elena, who also trusts me as much as I trust her. Both of them dig me from the hole of doubt over and over again in this crazy business. I'm insecure and anxious when it comes to my work and I appreciate their patience and encouragement. To all of Simon & Schuster, let's keep rocking.

In the story-maker category, I have to thank my childhood friends, who actually fuel so many of my stories. To Oxon Hill; and Washington, DC; and Brooklyn. To Aaron, and Ms. CeeCee, the best candy lady ever. To my folks, and my siblings. To the dogs we ran from. The bicycles and bus stops. The ice-cream trucks, and parking lot carnivals. Corner stores, and barbershops. To all the colorful neighborhoods, and all the colorful kids making the journey home.

I love you.

I like you.

I ask you:

How you gon' change the world?

LOOK BOTH WAYS:
A TALE TOLD IN TEN BLOCKS

by Jason Reynolds

Discussion Questions:

1. Jasmine says if she has to be something else, she would choose to be a water bear. *Water bear* is the common name for an organism called a *tardigrade*. Research these organisms online. What makes them unique? Why do you think Jasmine would want to be one? Would you want to be a water bear too? Explain your answer.

2. Jason Reynolds writes poetry as well as prose, and he has incorporated poetic language into this novel. As you read, look for examples of figurative language. For example, list all the similes you can find in the first chapter. How does the use of poetic language impact you as a reader? Why do you think a writer might choose to use this type of language?

3. Choose one of the chapters in the book and identify specific details in the text that develop the relationship between the characters in that chapter. What details does Reynolds reveal directly? What does he reveal indirectly? Examine the way other characters respond and speak to one another, as well as their thoughts, actions, and/or appearances.

4. Why do you think the Low Cuts only steal loose change? Explain how they use the money they collect in chapter two. What do their actions reveal about their values? Did your perception of them change once you knew how they were using the money?

5. Reynolds describes the Low Cuts as a "braid of brilliance and bravado." What does this description suggest about the group?

6. Why do you think Reynolds begins and ends the third chapter, "Bastion Street," with a series of statements that begin with the word *maybe*? What do you think would have happened if Pia and Stevie talked with each other?

7. Reynolds describes Pia's skateboard as her voice. What do you think he means by that? How are you

most comfortable expressing yourself? Do you prefer to use words or some other outlet?

8. Reynolds explains that Ty knows "the anxiety of a kind of war." What is the source of Ty's anxiety and confusion? Why do you think Bryson defends him? Have you ever felt similarly? If so, how did you handle those feelings?

9. How would you answer Benni's question if she asked you how you were going to change the world? What change would you like to see?

10. How does Simeon and Kenzi's street differ from other neighborhoods in the book? Why do you think the boys call themselves brothers?

11. Explain why Satchmo is afraid of dogs. Have you ever had a bad experience that caused you to fear something? Satchmo makes an elaborate escape plan to deal with his fear. What have you found that helps you face your fear?

12. Why do you think Cynthia considers her mother her hero? How does laughter help her and her grandfather deal with grief and loss?

13. How do you think Sandra responds to Gregory after she smiles? Explain your answer.

14. The final chapter begins with a string of metaphors describing a school bus. Choose two or three metaphors that you find especially effective, and explain what you think each metaphor you selected means.

15. Which one of the chapters did you like the best? Which character did you most relate to? Explain your answers.

16. Several of the characters in the book are victims of bullying or harassment; think about Pia, Stevie, Bryson, and TJ. How do these characters respond when they are bullied or harassed? Which character do you think deals with the problem in the healthiest way? What advice would you give someone who was being bullied or harassed? What steps could you take in your community to try to prevent this kind of behavior?

17. The subtitle of *Look Both Ways* explains that it is a "tale told in ten blocks." While each chapter in the book can be read as a stand-alone story, Reynolds uses repetitive images, settings, and characters to connect the stories. Identify one of these connecting devices and explain how it links the stories.

18. Although the characters in each story go to the same school and live in the same neighborhood, they don't really know each other or understand the struggles that their classmates face. If you could orchestrate a friendship between two characters from different stories, which characters would you want to be friends? Explain your answer. Do these interactions make you think any differently about classmates or friends in your own life? Is there someone whom you'd like to get to know better?

19. "Canton smiled, knowing a school bus is many things. So is a walk home." What do you think these last lines of the book mean? What does Canton realize after observing his classmates?

20. Why do you think Reynolds titled this book *Look Both Ways*? Can you think of different meanings for the title?

Guide prepared by Amy Jurskis, English Department Chair at Oxbridge Academy.

TURN THE PAGE FOR A PEEK AT
ANOTHER **JASON REYNOLDS** NOVEL,

as brave as you.

#460: POOP. POOP iS StuPid. StuPid POOP. StuPid. POOPid. POOPidity. IS POOPidity a woRd?

Genie stood a few feet away from Samantha's shabby old doghouse, scribbling a mess of words in his notebook. His older brother, Ernie, was luring the mutt to a cleaner spot in the yard with a big pot of leftover chicken, bacon, grits, greens, and whatever else was for doggy breakfast.

"Okay, that should keep her busy for a few minutes," Ernie said, successful. He walked over to the side of Grandma and Grandpop's house, grabbed a rusty shovel, then came back to Genie and started scooping up crusty piles of dog poop.

"What I wanna know is what you 'bout to do with that mess?" Genie asked, pinching and pulling his shorts out of his butt. Ma must not have noticed how much he had grown since the year before when she packed all his old summer clothes.

"If you put that notebook down, you'll see," Ernie said, holding the shovel out and walking toward the back of the house where all the trees were. When he got close enough to the wood line, he looked over his shoulder. Genie shoved the small notebook into his back pocket. "You watchin'?" Ernie called out, making sure all eyes were on him.

Genie hustled over. "Yeah." Ernie flashed a sly grin, one that worked perfectly with his dark shades. Then, without giving any kind of warning, he cocked the shovel back and flung it forward. The poop flew into the air and out into the woods, slapping against the trees and exploding.

"Ooh yeah!" Ernie cheered, holding his shovel up as if he had just scored a touchdown.

Genie gaped, his mouth falling open as Ernie came back to scoop up more dog crud. "You just gon' stand there, or you gon' get in on this?" Ernie asked, chin-pointing to the other shovel leaning against the side of the house.

No way was Genie going to miss out on slinging poop. On *poopidity*? No. Way. How often does anybody get to catapult doo-doo into a forest? Never. Genie ran and grabbed the other shovel.

"Get this one," Ernie said, stabbing at a gross mound, still stinky.

Genie grimaced, but he slid the shovel under the poop, grimaced again at the scratchy sound of metal on dirt, then lifted it and followed Ernie back to the tree line.

"Go for it," Ernie said, nodding.

Genie put one foot forward, holding the shovel as if it were a baseball bat and he was about to attempt the worst bunt in history. He whipped the shovel forward, but not nearly hard enough. The poop plopped down only about a foot away. It was a pretty sad throw, and it was way too close to being a situation where poop was splattered all over Genie's Converses. Yeah, they were already covered in dust, but dust is one thing, even mud he could handle, but dog poop? There's no coming back from that.

"You gotta *fling* it, Genie. *Fling* it." Ernie demonstrated with a few ghost flings. "You see that tree over there?"

Genie looked out at all the trees in front of

them and wondered which one Ernie was talking about. It was pretty much . . . a forest. Trees were everywhere. And Ernie wasn't really pointing at any one in particular. He just said *that tree over there* as if one of the trees had been marked with a sign that said THIS TREE, DUMMY. But Ernie was always on him about asking too many questions, so Genie just nodded.

"Watch and learn, young grasshoppa." Ernie held the shovel low, letting it hang behind him before hurling its contents into the woods. It splat against a tree. Perfect shot. It must've been the one Ernie was aiming for, because he threw his hands up in celebration again. "Bang, bang! Got it!" he howled. "Now, try again."

Genie picked up another clump, questions flying all over the place like those flies on the . . . poopidity. Why was there so much of it in the first place? Did nobody else care that there was mess all over the yard? When was the last time the yard had been poop-scooped? Genie tried to mimic Ernie's every move. He held the shovel low and let it drop back behind him a little so that he could get some good momentum. We're talking technique here. Sophisticated stuff.

"Aim for that old house back there," Ernie said, pointing into the woods. Genie focused and counted off. One, two, and on three, he swung his whole body, a kind of broke-down golf swing, the mess whipping from the shovel head. Genie definitely got some air on it this time! But he hadn't quite figured out how to aim it—Ernie left that part out. The poop zipped off behind him, slamming into a window in the back of the house. The *wrong* house. His grandparents' house.

"Genie!" Ernie shouted, his eyes bugging. And right after that came Grandma.

"Genie!" she called out. "Ernie! What in Sam Hill are y'all doin'?"

Grandma was the one who put Ernie and Genie on poop patrol in the first place, in case you were wondering. Neither one of them had ever had to shovel poop out of anybody's yard before, because first of all, in Brooklyn, most people don't have yards. And secondly, most Brooklyn folks just pick it up with plastic Baggies whenever a dog does his doo on the sidewalk. Not everybody, but the majority. But there were no sidewalks here in North Hill, Virginia. No brownstones with the cement stoops where you could watch the buses, ice cream trucks, and taxis ride by. Nope. North Hill, Virginia, was country. Like *country* country. And Genie and Ernie were staying there in a small white house on the top of a hill. Grandma and Grandpop's house. For a month. Like thirty *whole* days.

The boys had arrived two nights earlier after a long, cramped ride in the back of their dad's old Honda. Cramped at least for Genie, because Ernie, in a cheeseburger coma, had stretched out on the backseat as if it were his own personal couch, forcing Genie to be smushed against the window for most of the trip. Genie had thought about playing Pete and Repeat by mimicking Ernie's nasty snores, but then he realized it wouldn't matter because Ernie wasn't awake to get annoyed by it anyway. And that was the whole point of that game. So to take his mind off the discomfort of being trapped under Ernie's leg, stewing in the thick silence between his folks, who had managed to not talk to each other for the past four hours, Genie flipped through pages of his notebook—where he kept his best questions. Some had already been answered, and some were still mysteries. He landed on one that he had totally forgotten about—#389: do honey badgers eat honey?—then tried telling his parents about how he'd read on the Internet that honey badgers actually *do* eat honey and how many of them have been stung to death by bees because they wanted honey from the hive so bad. The toughest, craziest animal ever.

"They're like weasels or somethin'. But tougher, know what I'm sayin'? Like, they're small, but they ain't scared to get busy, even on lions," Genie had rambled. The fact that his parents had neither asked him about honey badgers, or even knew why he cared about them in the first place, never stopped him from offering up random info at random times. That was sort of his thing. He was different from Ernie in that way. Genie was the kind of kid who kept a small jacked-up notebook and pen in his pocket just so that he could jot down interesting things whenever they came. The point was to keep a list—a numbered list—of all the things he needed to Google, because to Genie, the more questions you had, the more answers you could find. And the more answers you found, the more you knew. And the more you knew, the less you made mistakes. Genie wasn't about mistakes.

Ernie, on the other hand, was the kind of kid who wore sunglasses 24/7 just to make sure everybody knew he was cool, and to him, the biggest mistake anyone could make was not to be. That, and not being able to defend yourself. As a matter of fact, one of the only times Ernie didn't wear his shades was whenever he was doing karate, which he had been learning since he was seven. He was a brown belt, or as he put it, a "junior black belt." Genie loved to watch Ernie's matches and tournaments, but not quite as much as he loved to watch *Jeopardy!* and *Wheel of Fortune*. Ernie, on the other hand, liked to watch girls. Genie liked to build model cars. Ernie . . . liked to watch girls.

"Boy, if you don't go to sleep, I'm a honey *your* badger," Ma had droned from the front seat after Genie finished telling her about the video he'd seen of a honey badger actually taking on a lion. She was staring out the window, and had been the entire time they'd been on the road. Genie sucked his teeth. That was when Dad adjusted the rearview mirror so that he could see Genie.

"Son, tell me something." He darted his exhausted-looking eyes from the rearview back to the road. "How much you know about sloths?"

"Sloths?" Genie thought for a moment. "Well, I know they're lazy, and they sleep all the time," he answered reluctantly, feeling the setup coming.

"Uh-huh," Dad said, flat. He glanced back in the mirror. "See where I'm goin' with this?"

Genie sucked his teeth again. He knew exactly where Dad was going with it. Straight to *Genie please be quiet and go to sleep* town.

But Genie didn't go straight to sleep, even though that was what his parents wanted. Instead, he stared out the window, like Ma, for about an hour, peering into the darkness, thinking about his girlfriend, Shelly, and his best friend, Aaron. He wondered if they were going to do all the things they always did in the summer, like play in the hydrant and buy rocket pops from the ice cream man, without him. If they were going to miss his rants and all his knowledge about random animals and insects, and if Shelly would be able to spot a bedbug like he had taught her. He wondered if Aaron would try to impress Shelly with his backflips (girls love dudes who can do backflips) and if she'd eventually fold to his flippin' charm and kiss him. Of course, if she did, it would be a loaner kiss, Genie decided. A kiss to make up for the fact that *he* wasn't there. Nothing real. Genie sat there thinking about all these things, annoyed by his brother's snoring, listening to his parents not say a word, totally unsure about what was going to happen when they finally got to Virginia. The only thing he did know for sure was *why* they were going to the country in the first place, why he and Ernie had to spend a whole month away from Brooklyn for the first time ever.

It all had to do with Jamaica. Well, really it all had to do with his parents "not saying a word." They were "having problems," which Genie knew was just parent-talk for maybe/possibly/probably divorcing. They said they needed some time to try to figure it all out. When his mother first told him about the "problems," all Genie could think about was what his friend Marshé Brown told him when her parents got divorced, and how she never saw her father again. When he asked his mother about whether he was going to have to choose which parent he wanted to live with, or if he and Ernie were going to have to split up too, all she said was, "No matter what, me and your daddy love you both. Always." But that didn't really answer the question, which made it clear in Genie's mind that "figuring it out"—which, by the way, was supposed to happen in Jamaica, the first vacation his parents were taking without him and Ernie—really meant figuring out which parent got which kid, which, of course, meant this would probably also be the *last* vacation his parents would be taking without them. And it got Genie thinking about who he'd want to live with, Ma or Dad, which led to him scribbling a list in the dark. Really, two lists.

#439

Living With dad

PRO: I'd be safe from fires and thieves.

CON: dad works all the time and is never home.

CON: so I probably wouldn't be safe from fires and thieves.

PRO: I could watch scary movies.

CON: dad can't cook.

CON: dad stinks almost all the time, because of work.

Living With Ma

PRO: She can cook, real good.

PRO: She never ever stinks.

CON: She won't let me watch scary movies.
CON: I don't know if she can protect me
    from fire and thieves.
CON: Which means I'd have to protect her, and
    I don't know karate!

Eventually, after going back and forth in his mind about who he'd want to live with, and messily jotting his thoughts in the notebook, the smooth, dark road hypnotized Genie, finally coaxing him to sleep. He hadn't even realized he had drifted off until he was awakened by the sound of tree limbs scraping the sides of the car. The Honda was bumping its way up a hill, and the limbs looked like long fingers on big stick hands trying to get in and grab him. It was still dark, Dad had his window cracked, letting some air in, and he had changed the music from slow jams to nineties hip-hop.

"We here?" Genie muttered, wiping sleep from his eyes. He looked out the window but couldn't see anything except branches. The car dipped and bucked every few seconds as Dad kept slamming on the brakes to avoid potholes.

"Jesus! This road is a mess," he fumed, turning the radio off so he could concentrate. Genie quickly patted the space beside him on the seat, searching for his pen. Once he found it, he flipped to the next page of his notebook. #440: does TURNiNG the Radio off heLP YOU dRive betteR? he scrawled as Ma turned to him and flashed a sleepy smile.

"Yes, honey, we're here." The skin on her face looked heavy, and Genie wondered if she had slept at all during the ride. Actually, the skin on her face had been looking heavy for a few months. Since her and Dad had the big blowup where she screamed, like *screamed* screamed, and told him that all his time went to work and the boys, but he could never seem to make time for her. Ernie and Genie had been outside having a snowball fight, and Down the Street Donnie, known for being a jerk, had covered a quarter in snow and zinged it at Genie. Zapped him straight in the eye. Ernie had run over to check on him and when he saw the coin, most of the snow knocked off, he commenced to karatisizing Down the Street Donnie, all the way . . . down the street. Meanwhile, Genie had run inside, his palm to his eye, and stepped right into Ma and Dad's crossfire over how she was feeling neglected. The swelling around Genie's eye eventually went away. But the heavy on Ma's face never did.

Anyway, the point was, Genie hoped Ma had gotten some sleep on the way to Virginia, because the one thing he thought he knew about Virginia, he was right about. It was *far*. Way too far to be awake the whole time.

Ernie, on the other hand, had slept the entire trip—was still asleep, his mouth hanging wide open in that way that made the bottom half of his face look like it was melting, his sunglasses lopsided, only covering one eye. Genie pushed Ernie's leg off him, but it snapped right back up to its place on Genie's lap as if it were spring-loaded.

"Ern, wake up," Genie said, jamming his fingers into Ernie's thigh. "We here." Ernie didn't budge. "Ern!" Genie cried out, loud enough for Ma to hear. She turned around and slapped Ernie's leg. He snapped awake, confused, fixing his shades and wiping spit off his chin with the bottom of his T-shirt.

As the car approached the top of the hill, the sound of a dog barking came out of nowhere. Genie pressed his face against the window. Was that Grandma and Grandpop's dog? What was it doing outside? Did they know it had gotten loose? Was Grandpop up this time of the night walking it?

"Ernie, you remember Samantha?" Dad asked,

cutting the engine a minute after cresting the hill.

Ernie craned his neck to see out the window, yawning. He had been to North Hill once before, a long time ago when he was four. Genie hadn't come with him because at the time he was still a baby. That was also the last time Dad had seen his father. It had been almost ten years. And Genie had no idea what *that* was about.

AS AN ADDED BONUS,
HERE'S A SNEAK PEEK OF

GHOST

AS WELL!

jason**reynolds**

NATIONAL BOOK AWARD
FINALIST

GHOST

RUNNING *FOR* HIS LIFE. **OR** *FROM IT?*

CHECK THIS OUT. This dude named Andrew Dahl holds the world record for blowing up the most balloons . . . with his nose. Yeah. That's true. Not sure how he found out that was some kinda special talent, and I can't even imagine how much snot be in those balloons, but hey, it's a thing and Andrew's the best at it. There's also this lady named Charlotte Lee who holds the record for owning the most rubber ducks. No lie. Here's what's weird about that: Why would you even want one rubber duck, let alone 5,631? I mean, *come on*. And me, well, I probably hold the world record for knowing about the most world records. That, and for eating the most sunflower seeds.

"Let me guess, sunflower seeds," Mr. Charles practically shouts from behind the counter of what he calls his "country store," even though we live in a city. Mr. Charles, who, by the way, looks just like James Brown if James Brown were white, has been ringing me up for sunflower seeds five days a week for about, let me think . . . since the fourth grade, which is when Ma took the hospital job. So for about three years now. He's also hard of hearing, which when my mom used to say this, I always thought she was saying "harder hearing," which made no sense at all to me. I don't know why she just didn't say "almost deaf." Maybe because "hard of hearing" is more like hospital talk, which was probably rubbing off on her. But, yeah, Mr. Charles can barely hear a thing, which is why he's always yelling at everybody and everybody's always yelling at him. His store is a straight-up scream fest, not to mention the extra sound effects from the loud TV he keeps behind the counter—cowboy movies on repeat. Mr. Charles is also the guy who gave me this book, *Guinness World Records*, which is where I found out about Andrew Dahl and Charlotte Lee. He tells me I can set a record one day. A real record. Be one of the world's greatest somethings. Maybe. But I know one thing, Mr. Charles has to hold the record for saying, *Let me guess, sunflower seeds*, because he says that every single time I come in, which means I probably also already hold the record for responding, loudly, the exact same way.

"Lemme guess, one dollar." That's my comeback. Said it a gazillion times. Then I slap a buck in the palm of his wrinkly hand, and he puts the bag of seeds in mine.

After that, I continue on my slow-motion journey, pausing again only when I get to the bus stop. But this bus stop ain't just any bus stop. It's the one that's directly across the street from the gym. I just sit there with the other people waiting for the bus, except I'm never actually waiting for it. The bus gets you home fast, and I don't want that. I just go there to look at the people working out. See, the gym across the street has this big window—like the whole wall is a window—and they have those machines that make you feel like you walking up steps and so everybody just be facing the bus stop, looking all crazy like they're about to pass out. And trust me, there ain't nothing funnier than that. So I check that out for a little while like it's some kind of movie: *The About to Pass Out Show*, starring stair-stepper person one through ten. I know this all probably sounds kinda weird, maybe even creepy, but it's something to do when you're bored. Best part about sitting there is tearing into my sunflower seeds like they're theater popcorn.

About the sunflower seeds. I used to just put a whole bunch of them in my mouth at the same time, suck all the salt off, then spit them all out machine-gun-style. I could've probably set a world record in that, too. But now, I've matured. Now I take my time, moving them around, positioning them for the perfect bite to pop open the shell, then carefully separating the seed from it with my tongue, then—and this is the hard part—keeping the little seed safe in the space between my teeth and tongue, I spit the shells out. And finally, after *all* that, I chew the seed up. I'm like a master at it, even though, honestly, sunflower seeds don't taste like nothing. I'm not even sure they're really worth all the hassle. But I like the process anyway.

My dad used to eat sunflower seeds too. That's where I get it from. But he used to chew the whole thing up. The shells, the seeds, everything. Just devour them like some kind of beast. When I was really young, I used to ask him if a sunflower was going to grow inside of him since he ate the seeds so much. He was always watching some kind of game, like football or basketball, and he'd turn to me just for a second, just long enough to not miss a play, and say, "Sunflowers are all up in me, kid." Then he'd shake up the seeds in his palm like dice, before throwing another bunch in his grill to chomp down on.

But let me tell you, my dad was lying. Wasn't no sunflowers growing in him. Couldn't have been. I don't know a whole lot about sunflowers, but I know they're pretty and girls like them, and I know the word sunflower is made up of two good words, and that man ain't got two good words in him, or anything that any girl would like, because girls don't like men who try to shoot them and their son. And that's the kind of man he was.

It was three years ago when my dad lost it. When the liquor made him meaner than he'd ever been. Every other night he would become a different person, like he'd morph into someone crazy, but this one night my mother decided to finally fight back. This one night everything went worse. I had my head sandwiched between the mattress and my pillow, something I got used to doing whenever they were going at it, when my mom crashed into my bedroom.

"We gotta go," she said, yanking the covers off the bed. And when I didn't move fast enough, she yelled, "Come on!"

Next thing I knew, she was dragging me down the hallway, my feet tripping over themselves. And that's when I looked back and saw him, my dad, staggering from the bedroom, his lips bloody, a pistol in his hand.

"Don't make me do this, Terri!" he angry-begged, but me and my mom kept rolling. The sound of the gun cocking. The sound of the door unlocking. As soon as she swung the door open, my dad fired a shot. He was shooting at us! My dad! *My* dad was actually shooting . . . at . . . *US!* His wife and his boy! I didn't look to see what he hit, mainly because I was scared it was gonna be me. Or Ma. The sound was big, and sharp enough to make me feel like my brain was gonna pop in my head, enough to make my heart hiccup. But the craziest thing was, I felt like the shot—loudest sound I ever heard—made my legs move even faster. I don't know if that's possible, but that's definitely what it seemed like.

My mom and I kept running, down the staircase into the street, breaking into the darkness with death chasing behind us. We ran and ran and ran, until finally we came up on Mr. Charles's store, which, luckily for us, stays open 24/7. Mr. Charles took one look at me and my mom, out of breath, crying, barefoot in our pajamas, and hid us in his storage room while he called the cops. We stayed there all night.

I haven't seen my dad since. Ma said the cops said that when they got to the house, he was sitting outside on the steps, shirtless, with the pistol beside him, guzzling beer, eating sunflower seeds, waiting. Like he wanted to get caught. Like it was no big deal. They gave him ten years in prison, and to be honest, I don't know if I'm happy about that or not. Sometimes, I wish he would've gotten forever in jail. Other times, I wish he was home on the couch, watching the game, shaking seeds in his hand. Either way, one thing is for sure: that was the night I learned how to run. So when I was done sitting at the bus stop in front of the gym, and came across all those kids on the track at the park, practicing, I had to go see what was going on, because running ain't nothing I ever had to practice. It's just something I knew how to do.

Looking for another great book?
Find it
IN THE MIDDLE.